Girl TALK

Best Friends

Have you seen all the
Best Friends
books?

Friends
FOREVER

Gill Smith

First published in 1998 by BBC Worldwide Ltd
Woodlands, 80 Wood Lane, London W12 0TT

Text by Gill Smith copyright © BBC Worldwide Ltd 1998
The author asserts the moral right to be identified as the
author of the work.

Girl Talk copyright © BBC Worldwide Ltd 1995

ISBN 0 563 38092 6

Cover photography by Jamie Hughes

Printed and bound by Mackays of Chatham plc

Let **Girl TALK** introduce you to the greatest bunch of Best Friends ever...

First there's

who's animal mad **Gemma**

Then her best friend

Lauren the school sports star

...you'll soon find out about her.

Anya

Best Friends

They spend loads of time with

Last, but never least is

is the new girl in the group **Cari**

Quiet

Sunita

She's desperate to be a fashion designer

For Emma, Stephanie and Kate

Chapter 1

As usual, chaos reigned in the Gordon household. It was nearly quarter past eight and the whole family were trying to have breakfast at the same time. The bright yellow kitchen was filled with the smell of crispy, sizzling bacon and burnt toast.

Gemma Gordon stared miserably at her breakfast, then pushed it away.

"What's wrong with you, Gemma? Back to school blues, is it?"

Gemma's mum paused in between scraping the charred surface off a slice of toast and frowned over her shoulder at the girl staring miserably at the rashers in front of her.

"Sorry, Mum, I can't eat this!"

"Whyever not?" replied Mrs Gordon, brushing

Friends Forever

Best Friends

stray crumbs off her black leggings. "You always have bacon on Mondays!"

Gemma took a deep breath, "I know, Mum, but on that TV programme last night, Dick King-Smith said that pigs are more intelligent than dogs, and we don't eat dogs, do we – not even slobbery, yappy ones like Bart next door! So I've decided, I'm going to become a vegetarian!"

"And who might Dick King-Smith be, when he's at home?" snorted Gemma's dad, Garry, as he burst back into the kitchen buttoning his dark navy overalls before grabbing the bacon roll which awaited him on the table.

"He's a famous author, Dad. He knows a lot about pigs…"

"And I know a good bit of brekkie when I see it, so eat up before I do!" replied Mr Gordon, hungrily. "You don't want to be a pasty-faced, sawdust-munching veggie, do you! Haven't you heard that carrots scream when you pull 'em up?"

Chuckling to himself, Mr Gordon clumped out of the kitchen with his half-eaten bacon roll, a faint whiff of engine oil lingering behind him.

Mrs Gordon frowned, pushing back her brown wispy fringe from her green eyes. "Don't get your dad going. You know what he's like when he gets started."

2

Gemma raised her eyes and shrugged.

"Mum! Mum! Why won't Gemma eat her breakfast?" A small, whiny voice came from halfway under the kitchen table. Lucy Gordon was just seven and was the bane of her older sister's life.

"Oh, shut up, pain!" snapped Gemma. She still hadn't forgiven her for what she'd done last week. Gemma had caught Lucy trying to take her pet rabbit, Thumper, for a ride in an old shoe box tied to the back of her bike.

"*MUM!*" wailed Lucy, ever more insistently, kicking the chair legs and just catching Gemma's shins.

"Owwww!"

Sighing heavily, Mrs Gordon strode across the kitchen and pulled Lucy's chair away from the table. "That's enough, you two! Come on, Gemma, get a move on. I bet Lauren is waiting for you and I've got to take Lucy to school!"

"Mum, *can* I be vegetarian?" begged Gemma, her bright blue eyes pleading desperately. "Will you tell Dad not to make me eat meat? *Please,* Mum…"

"We'll see. Now, get going – Mrs Standish won't wait forever!"

Gemma swung her rucksack onto her shoulder and hurried out of the back door. As she burst onto Adams Avenue, her thoughts turned to what lay ahead that morning at school.

It was the first day back after the Christmas holidays, and Gemma couldn't wait to catch up with her school friends. She even had to admit she was quite looking forward to her first maths class. The rest of her friends thought she was totally bonkers. They hated maths and couldn't work out why she liked it so much – especially her best friend, Lauren…

"Hurry up, you slug! We'll be late!"

Standing by a furiously revving car, a tall, blonde-haired girl in a new, red puffa jacket waved at Gemma.

"No need to shout, Lauren Standish!" Gemma retorted with a grin. She and Lauren had known each other since they were babies. In fact, their mums – Karen and Mary – had been best friends at school too. There wasn't a thing in the world that Lauren didn't know about Gemma and vice versa. They hadn't always lived side by side, but when the house next door to the Standishes had come up for sale two years earlier, the Gordons decided it would be nice to leave the house on the Maryland estate, over on the other side of town, and move in.

That was the same year that Gemma's dad had

left his job in the big Citroën garage in town to work for his old boss, Dave, in the arches by the station.

It had been a bit of a struggle at first but when Mary, Gemma's mum, decided to help out a few days a week with the book-keeping, everything seemed to fall into place. The only drawback was that sometimes the whole house stunk like the inside of an oil can.

But while her dad fixed up broken cars every day at the arches, Gemma's main ambition in life – apart from owning a pony one day – was to be a vet. There wasn't an animal within a few streets' radius that she wasn't on petting terms with. Even old Mrs Crick's snappy chihuahua, Nelson, wagged his tail when he saw her walking towards him. Gemma was always first to volunteer to look after Squeak, the school guinea pig, during the holidays, even if he did bite Thumper's ears and steal his food when they were let out together.

Diving into the back of the old Ford Escort, Gemma just had time to snap her seatbelt shut before Mrs Standish tore off down the road leaving a cloud of exhaust behind her.

"Still not asked Dad to look at the car then, Mrs Standish?" yelled Gemma over the snarl of the engine.

Friends Forever

"No time, Gemma!"

"We were supposed to have picked up Sunita five minutes ago," added Lauren with a smile.

Sunita Banerjee lived three streets away. Her dad owned the local video shop, so Sunita was always the first one to get the latest films – much to Gemma's envy. Mr Banerjee's mum, Indira, lived with Sunita and her parents, and she fussed over Sunita as if she was made of candyfloss. Sunita's big brothers Ganesh and Vikram could do what they liked, and old Mrs Banerjee wouldn't turn a hair, but as soon as Sunita as much as took one step outside the front door without her mother in tow, the old lady would throw her hands in the air, begin wailing in English and end up howling in Hindi.

Sunita was already standing on the pavement, anxiously clutching her neat leather satchel, her gran stood firmly next to her, staring down the street.

As soon as the rusty orange car came into view, Sunita ran to meet it.

"Ah Sunita, *beti*, don't rush so! You'll upset your

tummy!" Old Mrs Banerjee waved her arms in the air like a windmill in a storm.

"Must go, *Dadima!*" yelled Sunita, using the special Hindi term of affection the old lady loved. Sunita's long black hair danced merrily as she waved her goodbye. "See you later!"

Mrs Banerjee Senior muttered darkly to herself as Sunita disappeared inside Mrs Standish's car. "That girl, she has no dignity! I must speak to her father..."

"Hello Sunita!" chorused Gemma and Lauren. "How was the weekend?"

Sunita pulled the brown satchel out from underneath her. "Oh, fine – but Gran was up to her old tricks again! She had Veena, Mrs Pancham's granddaughter round, trying to matchmake her with Ganesh!"

"Oh, yuck! How *could* she?" exclaimed Lauren pulling a face. "Not soppy stuff, please!"

"Oh no!" laughed Sunita, the dimples in her round brown cheeks popping into view. "Mum thought the whole thing was hysterical 'cos Ganesh was far more interested in his new playstation. All Veena wanted to do was play my Boyz album!"

All of a sudden, the car skidded to a halt. A very new, bright blue hatchback had backed out of the sloping drive in front of them without stopping. "Hey! Watch out!" boomed Mrs Standish crossly.

A neatly cut, black-haired head poked out of the driver's window. It was Mrs Michaels, the mother of their old friend, Anya.

"Sorry! Oh, hello Karen, it's *you*!"

Mrs Standish rolled her eyes up to heaven as she always did when she was exasperated. She said it stopped her from swearing.

"Hello Sacha – I should have known it would be you," she smiled.

"Hi Lauren! Hi Gemma!" An equally neat, but smaller head with long dark hair emerged from the passenger's window. The pretty, delicately-featured face with slanting blue eyes broke into a smile.

"Hi Sunita!"

"Oh, hello Anya, fancy bumping into you!"

"Yes, almost literally, eh? Look girls, why don't you come round for tea tonight after school? We can swap first-day-back stories, and I can fill you in on all the latest gossip! Byeee!"

Anya Michaels waved a small, elegant hand out of the window as the car rocketed round and shot off in the opposite direction. Anya didn't go to Duston like the other girls, she went to Lady Margaret Regis, a private school in town.

Sunita smiled thoughtfully as the blue car

disappeared into the distance. "Latest gossip... I wonder what she's got to say?"

"Oh, *darlings*, only the very latest news that matters!" said Lauren, imitating Anya's polite, squeaky voice.

"Oh, that's not fair," said Gemma defensively. "Anya can be a bit of a snob sometimes, but she's nice, really. She was a brilliant friend when my Grandad died last year and she's always giving us stuff which she's hardly worn or played with."

Lauren reluctantly nodded in agreement. "Yeah, I know. And she's stood by us, too. I mean, when she went to Lady Margaret Regis, she could have dropped us."

Sunita fluttered her eyelashes. "Drop? Friends as cool as us?" The others laughed, and Sunita continued, "hey remember when Gran wouldn't let me go to the zoo with the rest of you? Anya phoned her up and persuaded her that it would be good for my schoolwork!"

Gemma smiled – Anya would probably be able to persuade a polar bear to take off its fur coat if she tried hard enough. "I wonder what she *does* have to say?" she muttered.

Friends Forever

At last, the car drew up outside the already crowded gates of Duston Middle School for Girls.

"Out you get!" shouted Mrs Standish. "I'll phone Anya's mum and make sure she picks you up this afternoon if you're going round there for tea. Be good now!"

Slamming the car door, Lauren waved at a small group of girls who were milling around the playground. "Hi Tania! Hi Katie! Look at this puffa jacket I got for Christmas! Cool, eh?"

Sunita frowned slightly as Lauren ran up to Katie and Tania excitedly. "I don't know, Gemma, can't Lauren see those two are only friends with her because she's captain of the football team?"

Gemma watched Lauren as she paraded up and down in front of her admiring audience, dancing around like a catwalk model. "Oh, she realises that, Sunita," smiled Gemma knowingly. "And she's also twigged that we'll be here for her long after those two creeps have oiled their way all over someone else!"

"Ugh, gross!" grinned Sunita.

"We are best friends after all," said Gemma, linking their two little fingers together to make their secret sign.

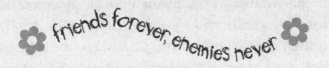

Sunita smiled back at Gemma as they let go of each other's fingers. It was so brilliant to have best friends.

The crisp morning air was suddenly filled with the shrill ringing of the school bell. Excitedly the girls piled into the warm, familiar classroom with the wide windows which overlooked fields on one side and the playground on the other. Last term's project papers were still pinned to the walls, but were somewhat dustier and more faded than they had been before Christmas. A lone piece of tinsel hung miserably from one corner of the room and the board still bore the message 'Merry Christmas, everyone' which Ms Drury, their form teacher, had written on the last day of term.

"Come along everyone, settle down!"

Right on cue, the tiny form of Ms Drury burst into the room, a large, multicoloured plastic bag bulging under one arm and her red hair loosely secured by the bright purple scrunchie she always wore.

Standing in the doorway behind her, looking as

if she wanted to disappear into the floorboards, was a small, mousy-haired girl with really untrendy pale pink plastic glasses. Peering into the noisy classroom, the girl scratched nervously at the small scab on her top lip.

"Woah! Nerd alert!" hissed a big, hard-faced girl who sat at the back. Alex Marshall and her two cronies, Charlotte and Marga made it their business to be as unpleasant as possible.

Ms Drury drew the small girl away from the doorway, putting one heavily braceleted arm around her shoulders. She was one of the more human teachers at Duston Middle School and always stood up for the quieter children.

"Class 6, this is Carli Pike," Ms Drury announced, as Carli nervously pushed her glasses up her snub nose. "She's joined us from Netheredge School and I want you all to make her feel *really* welcome."

"Pike! Of course... I know her," whispered Charlotte, a look of pure triumph spreading over her freckled features. "And we're going to have some right old fun with this one!"

Alex smiled to herself, her eyes narrowing like a hungry wolf. "Well girls, I think that sooner or later, Carli Pike is going to get a very special welcome to Class 6."

Charlotte and Marga sniggered, Alex's 'welcomes' only ever meant one thing...

Chapter 2

The first morning back soon passed. Whilst Sunita and Lauren scowled their way through maths, Gemma glowed as her nimble fingers danced over her calculator. She was almost disappointed when the bell sounded for break time.

"Honestly, Gemma, I just don't get why you like maths so much!" grimaced Lauren as the three girls walked briskly towards the playground.

"If that had been an art lesson, I could understand you getting a bit excited," added Sunita. "But maths, *yeuch!*"

"Yeah, but I'm hopeless with anything like that, Sunita! You're so lucky to be into sewing and stuff, you can make loads of cool clothes. I can't even stitch on a button!" said Gemma, poking her finger through the ripped buttonhole on her navy school cardigan. "Mum is always asking me why I can't be more like you!"

Sunita burst out laughing. "And my mum is always saying 'Sunita, forget all this dress-making nonsense. Why can't you be good at maths like your nice friend Gemma? You'll never make the grade as an accountant unless you can add up!'"

Suddenly, Lauren stopped in her tracks. "What's happened to the new girl, then?"

Gemma looked around the playground. Most of Class 6 were busy enjoying the mid-morning sunshine, but Carli Pike was nowhere to be seen. "That's funny, I thought she was following us out," puzzled Gemma.

"Shall we go back into the class and see if she's got lost?" suggested Sunita, turning back towards the classroom door.

The three girls tiptoed into the deserted classroom and there, sure enough, seated at her desk was Carli. "Oh, hi!" trilled Gemma brightly. "Aren't you coming outside with the rest of us then?"

Carli pushed her glasses up her nose and glared at her. "Please leave me alone!" she said, turning her face away.

"Oh... right, then," stammered Gemma, feeling a bit hurt.

Lauren pulled Gemma towards the door. "Come on, Gems, let's go back outside."

For the remainder of the break, Gemma was silent and withdrawn.

"Look, she's a nerd if she doesn't want to be friends with you!" cried Lauren, exasperated, as break ended. "You were only trying to be kind. If she's going to be like that, then I wouldn't bother with her!"

"Maybe," sighed Gemma, "but I didn't like the way that Alex and her crew were looking at her in class this morning. You know how they used to be with Sunita…"

"Until I stood up to them," Sunita replied. "Remember how she kept going on about how my skin was made of dirt until I reminded her, in front of the whole class, that she'd spent half of her summer holidays lying out in the sun trying to go the same colour as me!"

They walked back into the classroom. Carli was still sitting down by herself, miserably filling in her new exercise books.

"Maybe Carli's just shy," whispered Sunita as she opened her pencil case. "Perhaps she'll want to be friends when she gets to know us a bit better. It is only her first day after all."

Lauren irritably slapped her French book on the desk, ready for the next lesson. "Well, *I* think she

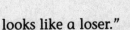

looks like a loser."

Gemma glared at her friend. She loved Lauren, but they didn't always agree. "How can you say that when you don't even *know* her?"

Lauren stared back at Gemma, feeling a touch uncomfortable. "Look, I just know, OK?"

Alex, Marga and Charlotte slowly made their way back to class. Even though the bell had stopped ringing to signal the end of break, they were still deep in conversation.

"So your Auntie Trish is going out with her dad?" said Alex, pushing her big, shiny face right into Charlotte's freckled one.

Charlotte smiled smarmily. "*More* than that – she's just moved in with him, in the next block to us! Poor old fish-face comes from a broken home!"

"Ahhhhh," sneered Marga, nastily.

"They're trying to keep it all quiet," went on Charlotte gleefully. "For poor little Carli's sake. They don't want people knowing what a lousy family she comes from!"

Alex led her cronies through the classroom door. She stared at the small, rumpled figure at the table in front of her who sat scratching the reddening eczema rash on her hands.

"Excellent, Charlotte. Most excellent," she gloated. "Don't forget, crew, special welcoming committee at home time."

Just then, Ms Drury burst into the room with a noisy clatter. "OK, girls," she trilled, pushing a hank of stray hair into the hideous purple scrunchie. *"Maintenant, nous parlons en français! Bonjour la classe!"*

Alex never made an effort in lessons, but she was particularly distracted by the thought of all the fun she could have with someone as pathetic as this little Carli.

"Alex, *repetez cette phrase, s'il vous plait!"*

Ms Drury's shrill voice echoed around the classroom. She tapped impatiently on the board where a very long French sentence had been written.

Alex's face became an unreadable mask. It was the face she used whenever she was confronted by an adult. She had perfected the art of never letting anyone see that they had caught her off guard.

"Sorry Ms Drury, I left my glasses at home and I can't see the board. Shall I ring my brother Zack on his mobile at lunchtime and get him to go and fetch them for me?"

The whole class groaned. Alex had two big brothers, Aaron and Zack, of whom everyone, including Alex's mum, were afraid. They were both tough nuts and the sight of a police car outside the Marshalls' house on the Fairlight estate was not unusual.

Sometimes when Alex wanted to really frighten someone, she'd get Zack to meet her from school. If a teacher ever challenged her, Alex would instantly look crumpled and say that her big brother had come to pick her up because she was frightened of walking home alone.

Ms Drury glared at her. "I don't recall seeing you in glasses before, Alex. Perhaps you'll bring them in tomorrow to show me?"

Alex glowered at her, and Ms Drury sighed. The teacher had long suspected that the big girl was not as innocent as she made out, and had tried, without success, to unmask her as the trouble-maker she believed her to be. In the privacy of the staff room, she often bemoaned the fact that there was a good brain going to waste under the tough, defiant exterior. Like all great liars, Alex was clever – she had to be to keep it all together.

The lunchtime bell sounded at long last.

"Phew! I'm glad our first morning's over," said Sunita. "It's time for *food*!" She opened her lunchbox and grabbed a pakora, made, of course, by Mrs Banerjee Senior. Gemma and Lauren sometimes brought their own food, but today, they plumped for the quiche and chips on offer in the canteen.

"I wonder where Carli is?" remarked Gemma, as the three girls tucked into their lunches.

"Oh, forget her!" said Lauren through a mouthful of chips. "She's probably hiding in some corner with the rest of the dweebs."

"Do you think we should have asked her to sit with us?"

Before Lauren could respond, Gemma spied a figure in pink glasses shuffling along the lines of chattering girls. "Oh look, there she is! Hey! Carli! Over here!" Gemma waved furiously, but the small girl refused to even look at her.

"*Carli*!" called Gemma again more loudly. She was determined not to be put off by the girl's lack of interest.

"Leave it, Gems, will you?" snapped Lauren.

"Why do you want to be saddled with her, anyway?"

Sunita put down her drink and frowned at Lauren. "Come on, don't be so mean." She turned to Gemma. "Gems, it looks like she wants to be on her own, so let's just leave her to it. After all, there are far worse things to worry about – like that English essay we were supposed to do over the holidays."

Lauren clapped her hand over her mouth as if to stop a scream. "Oh, rats! I've gone and left it at home!"

"Lauren, you'd forget your head if it wasn't screwed on," Sunita grinned as she packed up the remains of her lunch. "Come on, let's get some fresh air."

With that, the three girls got up and made for the playground. They passed by Carli who was sitting with a bag of crisps and a marmite roll. Gemma smiled, but she didn't look up.

"Hooray!" cried Lauren, throwing her books into the plastic box with her name on it. The clock had seemed to take forever to creep round to three fifteen, but they'd finally made it. In an instant the

21

friends had gathered up their homework and stuffed it into their bags. Sunita puffed as she struggled to fit the large maths book into her satchel. "Oh, I'll take mine home tomorrow," said Lauren loftily. "If we're going round Anya's, I don't want to lug too much about!"

"But my mum will pick us up, it's not like you've got to walk home!" laughed Gemma, combing her brown bob furiously. She didn't want to feel like a mess in front of Anya, who always looked as if she had just stepped out of a hairdresser's.

"And who are you tarting yourself up for, Gemma Gordon?"

Standing by the row of coat pegs in the corner of the classroom, with her two sidekicks in tow, Alex Marshall smiled greasily at Gemma.

"Mind your own, Alex," retorted Gemma. "Come on girls, there's a bad smell around here."

As she turned to go, Gemma caught Marga making a face at her, but she just shook her head and followed Lauren and Sunita out of the door.

"There she is, Alex!" whispered Charlotte, as Carli finally got up from her chair.

"Oi, fish-face!" sneered Alex, as Carli looked up. "Yeah, *you*!"

Alex slid over to Carli, towering over her. "Now, just in case you're in any doubt, I run the show around here and whatever I say goes, OK?"

Carli peered over her glasses, her hands shaking. "Wh-what?" she stammered, her voice barely a whisper.

Charlotte pushed in front of Carli, their noses almost touching.

"You do whatever Alex says, right, loser?" she hissed. "And if you don't, then I'll have a word with your dad Mike."

At the mention of her dad's name, Carli's bottom lip trembled. "Wh-what do you mean? You don't know my dad!"

"Oh yes I do!" sneered Charlotte, her breath steaming up Carli's glasses. "And what's more, if I tell him that your mum – now what's her name? – ah yes, *Susie*, sent you to school with only a packet of crisps for lunch, he'll soon have you taken away from her!"

"But she *didn't*! And you don't know my dad! You're lying!" sobbed Carli through her tears as she backed into a coat peg on the wall.

"Wanna bet?" added Marga, not wanting to be left out of the fun.

"What's all this, girls?" It was Ms Drury, coming back to investigate the raised voices. As usual she was loaded down with several carrier bags. Marga jumped away from Carli as if she had just given her an electric shock.

"Nothing, Miss. Carli just slipped and hurt herself on the coat peg and I was helping her up."

Gemma suddenly reappeared at the doorway – she'd come back in to get her homework diary. She took in the scene at a glance, but there was little she could do with Ms Drury around. She went to rejoin the others, going red as the anger mounted inside her.

Gemma caught back up with Lauren and Sunita in the playground, and told them what she'd just seen and heard.

"That's awful!" cried Sunita, looking shocked.

"Oh you know what Alex is like," said Lauren, "she can be all mouth sometimes."

"She certainly is *not*!" replied Sunita sharply. "Don't forget I'm not the only one she's made really unhappy."

Mrs Michaels waved at the threesome from her car window as they came into sight.

"Maybe Carli can handle it," suggested Lauren, doubtfully. The others looked at her, unconvinced.

No one spoke as they got into the car.

"We'll pick up Anya on our way home," said Mrs Michaels, her lilting voice with its slight Russian accent breaking the silence. "Is everyone all right? You're very quiet!"

"Oh, we're just tired out, Mrs Michaels," offered Lauren from the back seat.

"Not too tired, I hope! Anya is really looking forward to seeing you," replied Mrs Michaels.

But right now, Anya was the last thing on any of the girls' minds.

Chapter 3

"Eat up, Gemma! This isn't like you!" Mrs Michaels picked up a plate of sesame prawn toasts from a table almost creaking under the weight of such goodies.

"Sorry, Mrs Michaels, I've become a vegetarian." replied Gemma. "I can't eat anything with eyelashes."

Mrs Michaels put the plate back and looked puzzled. "Er, do prawns have eyelashes, dear?" Behind her, Sunita and Lauren couldn't contain their giggles. The pair of them exploded like over-shaken cola bottles, roaring with laughter.

"Tell me, Gemma," said Lauren, "does anything in chocolate cake have eyelashes? 'Cos if so, then that Mississippi mud pie is all mine!"

Anya sat on a pink velvet stool, fiddling with her long dark hair. "Prawns do have long, tendrilly things sprouting from their heads, Mum," she said, seriously, "and they *could* be eyelashes."

Gemma smiled. "Thanks for the support, Anya!"

Anya nibbled at one of the toasts herself. "That's all right. But I still think you're silly to miss out on something that tastes so yummy!"

Mrs Michaels picked up a folder from the other side of the room and sighed. "Well girls, I've got this article to finish so if I disappear for a while, you'll be OK, yes?"

"Of course we will Mum!" snapped Anya rather irritably, her pretty face souring. "We're not babies you know!"

As soon as Mrs Michaels had shut the living room door, Lauren pounced on the Mississippi mud pie. "Wow, we never have this at my house!" she exclaimed, heaping a huge wedge onto a big tartan plate.

"Great food!" agreed Sunita. "But, come on, Anya, what's going on? Any particular reason for this feast, apart from wanting to see your totally fabulous friends?"

Anya fluttered her long black eyelashes and tucked her feet neatly under the velvet stool. "We-e-ell..." she drawled, pausing to get their undivided attention, whilst casting her navy blue eyes upwards. "...You tell me about *your* day first!"

"Not a lot to tell, Anya," mumbled Lauren through mouthfuls of chocolate cake. "Ms Drury looks as horrific as ever and is *still* wearing the same awful scrunchie and, oh, there's this new girl called Carli who seems like a right nerd!"

"No she's not!" countered Gemma, speaking up for the first time. "She's just shy, that's all. I think she seems quite nice."

Anya loved gossip. She arched a neat, black eyebrow and leaned forward. "Where does she come from then?"

"She was at Netheredge school before she came to Duston," replied Lauren through chocolate-coated teeth.

Anya suddenly looked as if a small puppy had done something nasty right under her nose. "Ugh! How awful. She must live on that council estate, then. How s–a–d." She spat out the letters like they were the silver paper off the mini rolls.

"Well, not everyone's as lucky as you," said Sunita with a hint of sarcasm. "Anyway, come *on*! What did you want to tell us?"

Anya took a deep breath and began chattering excitedly. "OK, well, there were rumours at the end of last term, but it's all true! We've got this really cool new girl in our class. Her name is Astrid

Spencer and her dad, Terence, is this really famous artist! Her mum is so amazing too, she's called Tanith and she's just like Mystic Meg! Her dad was in the *Chronicle* the other week and guess what?"

Without pausing for breath, or a reply, Anya continued:

"The *Arts Today* show is doing a programme on him! And, even more mega, Astrid has asked me to come round when they're filming!"

The three girls looked at each other knowingly. Anya was famous for telling them that she'd been picked to do this or singled out to do that and then nothing ever came of it.

Lauren raised her eyebrows and giggled. "You mean, that her *dad* is that man in the paper with the drawings of ladies wearing nothing but fruit?" With that, she collapsed onto the floor, holding her sides and laughing so hard she turned beetroot red.

But even Lauren's amusement didn't stop Anya from chattering on like a demented parrot.

"Oh and guess what else? You know that panto that's on at the Grand Theatre? You *know*, the one with Claire Bryant and Darcus Edwards? Well, Claire Bryant is going to come to our school, coach us in singing and tell us all about life on the stage! What do you think of that?"

Gemma, who was more interested in the presenters of her favourite animal show, looked blankly at the small, animated figure in front of her. "Er, Anya, you've lost me there. Claire who? Is she famous or something, then?"

Anya looked at Gemma in disbelief. "Claire Bryant! You know, she's Cindy *in All Part of the Family* on TV, and Darcus has been in a West End musical!"

"So, when do we get to meet Astrid then?" asked Lauren, wiping her mouth with a napkin.

Anya stared at Lauren as if she'd just spoken to her in Turkish. "Sorry?"

"Yeah, when do we get to meet this wondergirl?" chorused Sunita, mischievously joining in the tease.

Anya shuffled on her stool, twiddled a lock of hair and looked down at her pretty slippers. "Um, well, it's just that Astrid is a bit shy... so why don't you leave her to me and I'll invite her round for tea next time it's my turn?"

The three girls glanced at each other. This was a familiar routine.

"What's the matter, Anya, is she too good for us?" asked Sunita, her dark brown eyes boring into Anya's shifty blue ones.

But just as Anya was beginning to turn slightly

pink, the front door bell clanged noisily. "Oh, that must be your mum, Gemma!" sighed Anya gratefully.

From the hallway came the familiar tones of Mrs Gordon. "Hi Sacha! Hope they've been behaving themselves!"

"Of course! And it's always a pleasure to have them round," replied Mrs Michaels, unaware that her daughter was squirming in the front room. "Some of those girls at her school are so unfriendly, she knows she's lucky to have such good friends elsewhere!"

The girls piled into the squat white van with *Arches' Autos* stencilled on the side in blue. Although Lauren and Sunita giggled about Anya's high and mighty antic Gemma was still quiet on the way home. As she looked out of the back windows, all she could see was Carli's lonely face. Her heart went out to the strange new girl.

The van crunched into the kerb outside the Gordons' house and Gemma vowed to herself that she would definitely make friends with Carli – no matter what *anyone* thought.

Chapter 4

It had been two whole weeks since Gemma had turned vegetarian. She had even stood up to both her dad waving sausages under her nose and her little sister Lucy's name-calling.

"Mum! Gemma's taking the ham out of her sandwiches!" cried Lucy, twisting herself out of her coat once more.

Mrs Gordon shook her head and tried again to fasten her daughter's buttons.

"Lucy, if you don't stop squiggling about you're going to be late for school!"

"But, Mum…" she insisted, whining.

"Oh, be quiet, pain!" snapped Gemma. "Why don't you go and suck on your dummy!"

"Gemma, that was really quite uncalled for," reprimanded Mrs Gordon as the small girl's lip started to quiver. "Now, say sorry to your sister – and would you please stop picking out that ham!"

"Sorry, Lucy," muttered Gemma, sulkily as she piled up the torn slices of meat.

Just then, the back door flew open and in burst Lauren, grinning from ear to ear.

"Hi, Gems! What on earth are you doing to your packed lunch?" Lauren peered closely at the newly-demolished sandwich on the breadboard and pulled a face. "Still into being a veggie, then? Well, how do you know that cheese doesn't have eyelashes? I mean, it comes from a cow, doesn't it? And they have eyelashes!"

Exasperated, Gemma pushed the two slices of bread with their squashed cheesy filling together and wrapped them in clingfilm. "Very funny," she grimaced. But there was no stopping Lauren...

"Well I heard that if you don't eat meat when you're a child, you don't grow properly!"

"I think you'll find that's not true," chipped in Mrs Gordon, putting Lucy's bag over her shoulder. "But one thing I do know is that you're *late*!"

"We're *always* late," sighed Gemma, with a rueful smile at her friend. "Full steam ahead, Lauren!" she cried, shoving her friend out through the back door.

The two girls sprinted full pelt towards Sunita's

Friends Forever

house. This morning, her mother was in charge of the school run. As they turned the corner of Adams Avenue, they could just see Mrs Banerjee in her blue padded jacket and jeans, getting into the car with Sunita.

"Hey! Mrs Banerjee! Wait for us!" shrieked Lauren, putting on a sudden spurt of speed.

"Lauren!" puffed Gemma, some metres behind her. "You forget I can't run as fast as you!"

Mrs Banerjee caught sight of the girls and waved out of the car window.

"Ah, *there* you are! Just made it, now hop in and we'll get you there on time!"

As the car rattled around the corner, Sunita pulled a wedge of drawing paper out of her bag. "Look you two, I wanted to show you this new gym kit I've designed!"

"Wow!" gasped Lauren, looking at the sheaf of papers covered with spindly models wearing finely-drawn outfits. "You're so good at this!"

Sunita glowed with pride. She liked nothing better than to spend her spare time designing clothes. It was what she wanted to do when she grew up.

"You'd be better off concentrating on your maths homework, Sunita!" said Mrs Banerjee grimly. "And you know how it upsets your grandma."

Sunita pursed her lips. Her gran had nearly had a blue fit when she'd found Sunita's latest designs. "But Sunny, you can see knees! That is most unseemly for a young lady. It might be all right for those hussies you like so much, but not for a young lady. *Sri Rama*! And to think that at that school they make you go outdoors where boys can see you! Young ladies should be doing graceful things, like classical dancing." Although Sunita loved the colourful Hindi films her dad brought home, she'd far rather learn a disco routine any day.

Sunita thought it best that she tell Gemma and Lauren all about her ideas later, out of her mum's earshot. Although Indranee Banerjee had been born in England and was pretty cool about Western stuff, there were certain matters over which she took her mother-in-law's side. Sunita's ambition to be a fashion designer was one of them.

As the school gates loomed into view, Gemma fell silent. She was still worrying about Carli and plotting how to win the girl over. She didn't dare share her feelings with Lauren, because she knew what sort of reaction she'd get.

As the three girls got out of the car, the morning bell was just sounding. "Oh no, we're in trouble!" yelled Sunita, dragging her bag out of the car boot. Lauren was already tearing through the school gates.

"Hold on, Lauren!" shouted Gemma. "You know we're not as fast as you!"

"Start training by catching me up, then!" called Lauren over her shoulder with a big grin.

The noisy buzz of chattering greeted the girls as they bolted through the door of Class 6. Ms Drury was fussing away in the far corner of the room, trying to pile up a heap of books and so didn't notice as they stole towards their places.

Just as Lauren sat down, she caught her finger in between the chair and the table leg and let out a howl of pain. Ms Drury whirled round in time to see Lauren biting her bottom lip whilst turning a dark crimson colour.

"Lauren Standish, do be quiet!" shouted Ms Drury, her wayward red hair escaping from its moorings and falling over her eyes.

"Sorry Ms Drury," grimaced Lauren.

"Phew, that was a close one," hissed Sunita under her breath.

"Right Class 6!" their teacher announced. "Today, I want you all to get up in turn and tell the whole class about your favourite hobbies. Seeing as how you look so happy, Sunita Banerjee, you can be first."

Now it was Sunita's turn to go red. She stood up, a little wobbly on her feet, and glanced around the room. At the back of the class Alex Marshall sat with her two sidekicks Charlotte and Marga. At first they watched Sunita smugly, but then they just stared disinterestedly out of the windows. Tania and Katie were huddled together, as always, at a table a few feet away by the classroom door whilst Carli sat by herself, knitting her inky hands together, at the end of a table with Mabel, Amy and Laura.

But any thoughts of Carli were soon swept away as Sunita started speaking. "Well, I've got some of my latest fashion designs here with me," she said, pulling a sheaf of papers out from her bag. "I get a lot of ideas from watching the Indian films which my Dad brings home. The stars wear lovely clothes and the colours are fantastic..." she told the class as she held up a page filled with bright sketches. "For this one, I imagined I'd been asked to design an evening outfit for the top Indian film star Jamilla – and this is the result."

"Well done, Sunita," said Ms Drury as she finished her presentation to the class. "I'm sure that one day I will be proud to say that the famous Sunita Banerjee was once a pupil of mine!"

Sunita flushed excitedly as she sat down. "Wow!" whispered Lauren admiringly. "That was ace!"

One by one, each girl got up and spoke. Lauren talked about football, Gemma spoke about her love of animals and even Alex shuffled to her feet and gruffly told everyone about how much she loved going skateboarding with her brother Zack.

Finally, Ms Drury looked absent-mindedly around the class as if she knew that she had forgotten someone. There, trying to squash herself ever smaller into her chair, was Carli Pike. Ms Drury's eyes lit up when she spotted the small, trembling figure. "Ah Carli," she smiled. "We haven't heard from you yet. As none of us know you very well, perhaps you'd like to get up next and tell us about what you enjoy doing."

Carli peered through her glasses and pushed them nervously back onto her nose. Her pale green eyes darted back and forth, as she started to scratch her right hand furiously.

"Come on, now! We're all dying to hear from you!" said Ms Drury, patiently.

Carli hung her head and fixed her eyes on the floor, not budging an inch from her seat. The teacher looked expectantly at the mousy-haired girl and frowned. She could see that Carli was near to tears and thought better of forcing her to stand up.

"All right then, Carli, maybe another time?" said Ms Drury, turning to the whiteboard and writing the words 'homework' on it in blue letters.

"Well, what do you think of that, then?" whispered Sunita. "I think our new girl is a bit of a mystery!"

Lauren wrinkled her nose and tossed back her long blonde hair. "A bit of a *dweeb*, you mean!"

Gemma shot Lauren an impatient look. "Why is it that you always are so mean about people who are shy?" she said, clearly put out.

"Oh, get over it," said Lauren, tetchily. She really couldn't understand why Gemma had started defending Carli the whole time.

The two friends ignored each other for the rest of the lesson, but at breaktime, Sunita slipped an arm round each of them. "Come on, you two, there's no point falling out over this."

"I guess not," agreed Gemma, offering out her little fingers. With a smile, Lauren and Sunita linked hands with her and chanted their special words.

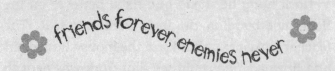
friends forever, enemies never

"That's better," grinned Sunita. "Now, who wants something from the canteen?"

"Not me, thanks," said Gemma.

"I'll come with you," offered Lauren. "See you in a minute, Gems!"

Gemma felt better as she went for a walk around the playground, now that she'd made up with Lauren. All around her, groups of girls chattered or sang their favourite pop songs together. Only Alex, Marga and Charlotte looked bored, lurking menacingly under the trees.

Just then, she saw Carli appear from the school building, blinking nervously at the hectic scene in front of her. With a nudge, Alex signalled to Charlotte and Marga. The three girls strolled across the playground towards Carli, who was standing against a brick wall.

"Oh no," muttered Gemma, her heart sinking, jogging over towards them.

"Hiya home-alone kid!" sneered Charlotte in a loud voice. "So when are you being taken into care then?"

Alex and Marga burst out laughing and jostled

Carli as they walked past. Carli tried to hold onto the wall, grazing her hand that was already reddened by her frantic scratching. Charlotte pushed her back against the bricks, and tears filled Carli's eyes as she broke into a run to get away from her tormentors.

In her confusion, Carli pelted straight towards Gemma. Gemma grabbed hold of Carli's thin, cheap cardigan, trying to keep her balance. "Hey, Carli! *Wait*!" she cried.

Carli turned round, fear obvious in her green eyes, tears streaming down her face. She jerked her cardigan free from Gemma's grasp, lashing out in all directions, just as Ms Drury walked into the playground.

"Just leave me alone, will you!" Carli shouted, her reedy voice silencing the break-time chatter.

Ms Drury didn't spare a second. She marched purposefully up to Gemma, an audience gathering behind her. "What on earth are you doing, Gemma Gordon? I will not have bullies in my class! Report for detention tomorrow lunchtime in the Head's office!"

Gemma looked at Ms Drury, shocked beyond words. She had never seen her teacher so angry.

She, of all people, hadn't meant Carli any harm, but now Gemma was being blamed for

41

bullying when it was Alex and her friends who were responsible!

"But, Miss!" she began, her mouth dropping open in utter horror. "I wasn't bullying her!"

"No arguments. The Head's office, tomorrow!"

Sunita and Lauren stared on in shock, having come back out in time just to see Gemma frantically tugging at Carli's jumper.

"That didn't look good," said Sunita. "But surely Ms Drury must know Gemma would never bully anyone?"

Lauren glared over at Alex and her cronies, her mind racing. While Carli cried her eyes out, they were practically crying with laughter.

Chapter 5

Weekends meant only one thing in the Standish household – *football*. Bart, their daffy mongrel who was part labrador but thought he was part human, loved weekends best of all. He bounced about with an old boot in his mouth, tail wagging furiously, looking forward to plenty of running around outside.

"Karen! Two pairs of shorts are missing, have you seen them?" Mark, Lauren's dad, yelled up the stairs.

Mrs Standish's blonde head appeared above the banisters, an irritated expression on her face. "No, I thought that you had them!" she replied as Ben, her eldest son, swung past her, leaping down the stairs.

"Mum, we're going to be late if we don't get a

move on," Ben moaned, just managing to avoid stumbling over the large blue sports bag that was at the foot of the stairs. "Who put that there?" he grumbled as he picked it up. "Lauren! I'm going to kill you!"

"What now?" At the mention of her name, Lauren came zooming out of the kitchen clutching a half-eaten slice of toast and honey. Without pausing to look where she was going, she collided straight into her brother.

"OWW!"

The pair fell over, a tangle of arms, legs and football kits.

Mrs Standish came down the stairs carrying little Harry. She found Lauren and Ben on the floor, with Bart joyfully nipping their heels. Mrs Standish took a deep breath and silently counted to ten.

"Right, you two, get up this instant!" she barked, as calmly as she could manage.

But just as Lauren stood up, Harry, thinking this was all a great new game, grabbed a chubby fistful of his sister's long blonde hair and pulled with all his might.

"OWWWWW!" yelled Lauren, even louder. "Get off, will you?"

Harry's face broke into a huge smile. "Funny

Lawen!" he cooed.

Lauren looked at the toddler fondly, peeling his fingers off her ponytail. "Honestly, Mum, what are you feeding him? He's so strong he could take on the whole team by himself!"

"Don't I know it," chipped in Mr Standish. "He nearly tugged off my moustache the other day!"

Eventually Lauren's mum tracked down the missing shorts, sending Mr Standish outside to start the car. "Come on everyone!" he shouted, tooting the horn so loudly that Mrs Crick across the road twitched her net curtains to see what all the fuss was about. "Hurry up! Only half an hour to kick off!"

Twenty minutes later, the car drew up outside the sports centre where Mr Standish worked. Lauren suddenly felt jittery as she always did before an important match. But, today, she knew that Sunita's big brother, Vikram, was going to be playing too. Lauren idolised Vikram – he was just about the best football player in the district and it was rumoured that scouts from nearby Lupton

Friends Forever

Town FC were interested in him already.

The family piled out of the car. Lauren ran on ahead, eager to get into her kit, leaving Bart running joyfully around Mr Standish as he unloaded the car. "See you later, Lauren!" he called after his disappearing daughter.

In the girls' changing room, the team were getting ready. Tania preened herself in the mirror, tucking her blonde curls into a bright hairband. "Hey, you're not going onstage, it's a football pitch you're playing on!" yelled Lauren across the room.

Tania reddened. "But, Lauren, I was only..." she began.

"I know, I know," said Lauren, with a smile. "But out on that pitch it's football first, fashion second, OK?"

Tania nodded quickly.

The team were playing today on the large, indoor pitch. Upstairs in the spectators' gallery, Mrs Standish sat with Harry attached to a long rein. He could just about see over the rails and ran excitedly up and down the gallery as far as his harness would let him. Ben sat around, impatiently waiting for his own game to begin, while Mr Standish, who looked after the facilities at the leisure centre, was busy checking everything was running smoothly.

Seconds before the match was due to begin, Vikram Banerjee appeared in the gallery wearing his tracksuit. He wasn't playing either until after the girls' heat.

"Hi Mrs Standish!" he shouted.

"Hello Vik! Nice to see you!" said Mrs Standish beaming back. She, too, liked the tall, wiry boy with his neat, black hair and eyes just like his sister's. "Come to cheer on Lauren, have you?"

Vikram smiled. "She's a great player, Mrs Standish. In fact, she's better than most of the boys her age. We could do with someone like her in the under Eleven's five-a-side but they won't allow girls in – *yet!*"

The game was an exciting one. The two sides were evenly-matched and Lauren's team had to work hard. Then just before the end of the second half, with the score at one all, it happened.

Lauren was just about to shoot for the goal, when one of the other team tackled her. Lauren sprinted up the pitch, desperately trying to get the ball back, but ended up kicking the girl in the shins. Her opponent made a huge show of falling over and clutching her leg, howling in agony. Lauren knew that it was an accident but the referee – who was known to be tough – took the other girl's side and awarded her team a penalty. Lauren saw red. She couldn't help herself, and stormed over to the referee, fuming.

Up in the gallery, Mrs Standish covered her eyes. "*Please* don't do it Lauren," she whispered to herself.

"Are you blind?" raged Lauren, turning purple. "It was an accident!"

The ref, who was a rather sour-faced, balding man eyed Lauren sternly. "I have to warn you, young lady, any more of this and it's the yellow card!"

"But I didn't mean to hurt her! She's making a fuss over nothing! Any fool can see that!" protested Lauren, not wanting to let it go. "Are you blind, or what?"

The referee's eyes bulged like gobstoppers. He turned pink, then puce before pulling the dreaded red card out of his pocket. "Never mind the yellow card, you, young lady, are *booked*! Off you go!"

Lauren stared at the red card held right under her nose. Hot tears sprang to her eyes.

"I said *off*!" yelled the ref. There were murmurings of disbelief from her team mates as Lauren slowly walked off the pitch, her head bowed low.

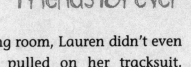

Back in the changing room, Lauren didn't even stop to shower. She pulled on her tracksuit, grabbed her bag and made for the gallery where she knew her mum was waiting.

As she pelted up the stairs blinded with tears, she ran into Vikram who was on his way to the boys' match.

"Bad luck, Lauren!" he said, a concerned look on his face. "That ref was out of order, anyone could see that that girl was faking it!"

Lauren looked at Vikram and wanted the ground to swallow her up. She felt embarrassed beyond words that her hero had watched her lose her rag and get sent off.

Without saying anything, she hurried past him and through the gallery doors. Baby Harry toddled towards her, his little arms held out in front of him.

"Lawen! Lawen!" he smiled, but Lauren rushed past him, straight into her mum's arms.

"Oh, Mum, why do I lose my temper so badly?" she sobbed. "And in front of Vik too!"

Mrs Standish smoothed down Lauren's tangled hair. "Come on, don't get too upset, it was clear to everyone that you weren't at fault…"

"But I made it worse!" cried Lauren, her face a red, blotchy mess. "I really let my side down!"

"You didn't mean to," soothed Mrs Standish,

standing up and reeling Harry back in. "Let's go and have a hot chocolate in the café and then we'll go and find the others, eh?"

Lauren nodded miserably. She couldn't imagine ever feeling worse than she did now.

Back at home that afternoon, Lauren still felt down. The ref had judged her just as Ms Drury had done with Gemma earlier in the week – he'd quickly made up his mind about something but had got it wrong. Except that when it happened to her, Gemma hadn't gone berserk and made things a hundred per cent worse. She'd accepted the situation, even though it was totally unfair.

Lauren smiled at the thought of her best friend, and decided to go next door and see her. Gemma always gave good advice and would definitely understand.

Lauren unlatched the gate to the Gordons' back garden. In the corner, by the far wall, Gemma was busily cleaning out Thumper's hutch.

"Hi Lauren," she called. "How did the match go?"

Lauren hung her head. "Er, I got sent off."

Gemma put down the straw she was holding and looked closely at her red-faced friend.

"Oh Lauren, don't tell me you lost your temper – again?"

Lauren kicked a stone down the garden and told Gemma the whole story. "What's worse," she concluded, "is that Vikram saw the whole thing. Oh Gemma, he'll never take me seriously as a football player if I go around losing it all the time!"

Gemma sighed and picked up the big grey rabbit who was snuffling on the grass beside her.

"Look Lauren, why are you so worried? From the sound of it, he doesn't think that you were out of order. He said that, didn't he?"

Lauren brightened up visibly. "Yeah. You're probably right, but…"

"But nothing. Come on, forget it," said Gemma. "I've got to give Thumper his supper now, but after that, why don't you come in and have some tea with me? Mum's left us some lovely vegetable nuggets and nettle salad!"

Lauren pulled a face. "Ugh, is Thumper eating with us too? Honestly Gems, haven't you given up on this veggie lark yet? I think it's stupid!"

"Er, *hello* – joke?" said Gemma, tapping on Lauren's head and smiling. "Anyway, Sunita says that lots of men in India are vegetarian. In the

South, hardly anyone eats meat! Half a country can't be stupid, can they?"

As Thumper settled down to a juicy piece of lettuce, the two girls went inside.

"Hey, I almost forgot – Anya phoned this morning," said Gemma.

"Oh yeah?"

"She says that her new friend Astrid has invited her over to tea tomorrow, so she won't be going round to Sunita's to see the video with us. She also mentioned that she'd be rehearsing with her for those new singing classes after school."

The tall blonde girl wrinkled her nose. "Are you sure this isn't one of Anya's stories, Gemma? Anya can't sing for toffee!"

Gemma looked at her friend. She knew that Lauren wasn't going to like what she was about to ask her.

"Lauren…" she began nervously. "I thought that maybe it would be nice to ask *Carli* if she fancied coming over instead. Mum knows where she lives – I found out that she and Carli's mum used to go to the baby clinic together when Lucy was tiny. I thought I could ask Mum to pick her up or something."

Lauren stared at her friend, a slow pink flush spreading over her face. "Haven't you got into

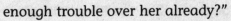

enough trouble over her already?"

"She was scared stupid!" protested Gemma. "She didn't mean to get me done by Ms Drury."

"But Gems, anyway…" Lauren sighed. "She just doesn't fit in with us. I mean, I know I'm always going on about Anya, but I really like her – she's the coolest-looking girl I know. But no way am I spending an afternoon with a boring, scabby loser like Carli!"

"Well, that's just mean, Lauren. She doesn't have any friends, Alex has put her at the top of her hit list, and I think the least we can do is try to make friends."

"And get another detention? Well, if that's the way you feel, then ask your precious Carli along, but count me *out*!" fumed Lauren as she turned sharply on her heel and stormed out.

Gemma watched her go, feeling completely torn. She wanted to help Carli, but she hated rowing with Lauren. If she could only make Lauren see that she was wrong about Carli, perhaps she'd be OK about including her in the gang.

Walking slowly back inside the house, she hatched a plan. As Carli wasn't on the phone, she'd go and see her this afternoon and invite her over anyway, without Lauren knowing. She was

sure Lauren would see that Carli was OK if she could just get the two of them together.

Gemma smiled to herself. Yes, that was the perfect way to solve both problems. She would go and see Carli straight after tea.

Chapter 6

"I won't be long, Mum! I'm just going out on my bike!"

"Okay, love, see you later."

Gemma Gordon wheeled her bike through the back gate, a guilty look shadowing her face. If her mum knew that she was going anywhere near the Fairlight estate without asking, she'd be in big trouble.

Pedalling furiously, Gemma sped along the narrow paths and through the park. She shivered inwardly as she saw the tall, grey towers of the estate looming in front of her. Row upon row of flats sat on top of each other. It reminded Gemma of the place she used to live in years ago.

Stopping as she reached the bottom of the sloping walkway which led up to Carli's block, she could hear the shouts of a group of boys somewhere nearby. There were some really tough kids in this area, and she started to feel nervous.

Taking a deep breath, Gemma got off her bike and pushed it along the walkway. She couldn't risk leaving it outside the block, because if it got stolen there was no way that she'd be able to explain *that* to her mum.

At the end of the walkway was a steep flight of stairs. How on earth was she going to get her bike up there? Grimly, she grasped it by the saddle and mounted the first flight of steps.

At last, exhausted and sweating, Gemma came to the second floor where Carli lived. She looked with bewilderment along the corridor of identical doors and wondered which one might be Carli's. She knew that the Pikes lived at number 25, but some of the heavy black doors didn't have numbers on.

She advanced slowly down the corridor, breathlessly counting up the flat numbers. "20...21... this one must be 22, and this one 23." She suddenly realised that number 24 didn't seem to exist and the next flat was number 26!

By now, Gemma's nerve had almost gone. She paced up and down the corridor, but it seemed hopeless. Beads of sweat broke out on her forehead and her hair clung to her face, making her even hotter.

As Gemma counted along the doors for one last time, she noticed that one of them had an old piece of paper taped to its window. On it was a number written in faded blue ballpoint – 25!

"That was close," she muttered, knocking smartly on the grimy black door.

There was no reply, so she banged again. After what seemed like an eternity, she heard the rattle of a door chain. The black door swung open just far enough for a woman's face to become clear.

"Yes?"

Gemma peered through the crack in the doorway. This was obviously Carli's mum. She had the same pale green eyes and snub nose, the only difference was that her hair was bleached bright blonde.

"Mrs Pike?" began Gemma nervously. "I'm a friend of Carli's. Is she in?"

Mrs Pike undid the chain and opened the door wide. She was small and neat, and wore tight blue jeans and a black cropped top. She looked more like Carli's big sister than her mum.

"Sorry dear, she's gone to the Grand Theatre with her Auntie Michelle to see a pantomime. But don't stand out there, come in! Our Carli didn't tell us that she had a new friend!"

Mrs Pike spoke with a slightly northern accent and had a kind smile. Gemma liked her immediately.

"And you'd better bring your bike in – otherwise it won't be there when you leave."

Thanking Mrs Pike, Gemma carried her bike into the flat. The smell of cooking and furniture polish hit her. Inside, the place was clean, but badly in need of a new coat of paint. There were scratches along the length of the wallpaper in the hall and piles of coats and boots were heaped over a fridge which sat at the end of it. Gemma looked at it in amazement. She had never seen a home with a fridge in the hallway before.

Gemma leant her bike against the coats, and Mrs Pike led her into the living room. Sitting in front of a Disney video was a small girl of about Lucy's age. "This is Annie, Carli's little sister. Annie, this is Gemma, a friend of Carli's."

Annie didn't look away from the television. She was too busy with the adventures on screen to bother with their visitor.

"Would you like a drink?" said Mrs Pike walking into the tiny kitchen at the end of the room. "Something fizzy, or orange squash?"

"Squash please," replied Gemma. She looked at the cracks in the walls and the old wallpaper and suddenly realised how lucky she was to have a nicely decorated house. The kitchen, she thought, seemed too small for Thumper, let alone a whole family.

Mrs Pike walked out of the kitchen carrying two plastic glasses.

"Thanks!" said Gemma. She took the drink and sat down on the edge of the sofa.

"It's so nice that Carli is making new friends," began Mrs Pike. "She had problems at her last school with bullying and stuff. In the end, we had to move her to Duston." Mrs Pike looked closely at Gemma and frowned. "You know, it's been tough for her over the past year since her dad left us. It's not been easy for me to make ends meet, but Carli's been brilliant about it. She never asks me for anything, no matter how many new clothes and treats the kids around her all get."

Gemma pictured Carli at her old school, being picked on, probably by some nasty piece of work like Alex Marshall. And on top of all that, she had to cope with her parents splitting up. Gemma could feel a lump in her throat – just the thought of her mum and dad not living together made her feel scared and tearful. She couldn't imagine how terrible Carli must feel.

Gemma gulped down the sickly sweet orange squash. "I'll make sure she's OK, I promise. Does

Carli still see her dad?"

Mrs Pike's face took on a pinched look. She bit her bottom lip, and Gemma wondered if she had asked the wrong thing.

"Not as much as any of us would like, Gemma," she said. "You see, Mike – that's Carli's dad – he's living with a woman called Trish on the other side of the estate. She's got a niece your age, Carli's met her now she's at Duston – Charlotte, is it?" Mrs Pike tilted her head on one side and looked searchingly at Gemma.

So that explained how come Charlotte seemed to know so much about Carli. "Oh yes," said Gemma. "I know Charlotte." She drained her glass. "I'd better be going now Mrs Pike, or my mum will worry. Will you tell Carli that she's invited round to my friend Sunita's house tomorrow afternoon to watch a video? Her dad has a video shop and he gets all the new films first. Maybe Carli could come to my place beforehand – we could go together. I've written down my address on this bit of paper."

"OK pet," said Mrs Pike, a little crestfallen. "But do come again, won't you? I'll tell Carli as soon as she gets in."

Wheeling her bike back through the estate, Gemma's mind was in a whirl. Everything made sense now…

Meanwhile, over at the Grand Theatre, Carli was having a vile time. She loathed pantos, she hated crowds and she absolutely couldn't stand loud music. Yet here she was, with her Auntie Michelle who was waving the glittery wand she'd bought in the foyer and showing her up no end. Auntie Michelle was her mum's younger sister and she loved parties and going out. She was always taking her niece on outings – and usually had a better time than Carli, who would rather have been at home, sketching.

The panto was the talk of Northborough. Everyone had been so excited when it was announced that Claire Bryant and Darcus Edwards were going to be starring in *Cinderella* at the Grand Theatre. There had been a massive rush for tickets and Michelle had only managed to get some because she used to work in the production office there.

All through the show, Auntie Michelle sang, danced and clapped loudly at the end of each song, much to Carli's intense embarrassment. She didn't think things could get any worse, but she was wrong – as the pantomime finished, her aunt yanked her arm bellowing excitedly, "*Come on*

Carli, get up and cheer!"

As the applause reached deafening levels, Carli slouched low, wishing she could become invisible, her hands covering her ears to block out the noise.

"I've got an even bigger treat for you now," said Michelle, nearly bursting with enthusiasm herself. Carli was suddenly hopeful – perhaps they were going to a restaurant for pizza or something – she rarely ate out, as her mum couldn't afford it.

She looked up at Michelle, eyes wide through her glasses.

"I phoned my friend Vicki who works in the press office, and guess what? We've got passes to go backstage and meet the cast! Isn't that great?"

Carli's heart sank. She was so shy that meeting new people seemed far worse than going to the dentist. And as for *famous* people...

But Auntie Michelle was now in full swing. She stood up, dusted the glitter off her dress and waved her wand over Carli's head dramatically.

"You *shall* go to the ball!"

Carli thought she was going to be sick. Oblivious, Michelle grabbed her hand and dragged her through the crowds. Everyone was pushing and shoving to get out. Carli clung to her aunt for dear life and shut her eyes.

Eventually they reached the backstage door and

were shown through a series of twisting corridors to a smallish room with a long mirror along one side. Carli stared from behind Michelle. A few people were clustered around, mainly with children in tow. An extremely pretty girl with long dark hair sat quietly over on the far side of the room with her nose in the air, her equally attractive mother by her side. There were plates of snacks on the table and cans of fizzy drinks, plus a few bottles of wine.

"Isn't this wicked?" Auntie Michelle was smiling like a Cheshire cat. Her big white teeth looked like tombstones under the bright lights. She adored the theatre, and wished she'd never left it to work at the newspaper offices in town.

At last, the door swung open and in breezed Claire Bryant and Darcus Edwards. Carli looked at Claire and gasped. She was every inch a princess, even when she was wearing everyday clothes. Her blonde hair shone and her big blue eyes sparkled confidently, greeting the crowded room. She looked amazing in a pair of really cool black trousers and a blue satin blouse. Claire smiled brightly in their direction, but Carli just stared at her feet.

The pretty dark-haired girl on the other side of the room rushed over to Claire and tugged at her sleeve. She thrust a blue notebook under the woman's nose. "Excuse me, Miss Bryant, can I have your autograph please?"

Claire Bryant signed her book quickly, then handed it back with a polite nod. As she looked around the room, she kept noticing the shy girl in the glasses looking utterly lost, and thought she would go and speak to her. The dark-haired girl's face clouded over with pure jealousy as Claire made a beeline for Carli.

"Hello there!" she said, the same musical tinkle in her voice as when she sang. "And what's your name?"

Auntie Michelle positively glowed with pride. She grasped Carli by the arm and hugged her proudly. "This is my niece Carli, and she's fab!" she gushed. "She's your biggest fan, just like me."

Carli wanted to die. Auntie Michelle had gone too far this time. Claire Bryant knelt down by the blushing girl and smiled kindly at her.

"Did you enjoy the show? I do hope so!"

"Of course she did, she loved it!" replied Auntie Michelle, before Carli had a chance to answer.

Claire looked thoughtful for a moment before asking, "Tell me, Carli, do you go to school round here? Only I'm going to be visiting a local one, soon."

The dark-haired girl was still loitering behind Claire and she looked like she was going to

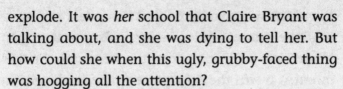

explode. It was *her* school that Claire Bryant was talking about, and she was dying to tell her. But how could she when this ugly, grubby-faced thing was hogging all the attention?

"I think it's the Lady Margaret Regis school," continued Claire. "Is that yours?"

Carli shook her head silently. Claire Bryant stood up and touched Carli's head ever so gently.

"Never mind, Carli. I'm so glad we met. Perhaps we'll see each other again some day."

With that, she walked over to the other side of the room. Darcus had been trying to get her attention and it looked as if even more people had arrived to see her.

The elegant dark-haired mum pulled her identical daughter to the exit. "Come on, Anya. It is so hot in here, we really should leave. Dad will be waiting outside to pick us up and we don't want him to get a parking ticket, do we?"

Anya's mouth was drawn in a tight, thin line. She was furious. How dare this awful girl talk to Claire Bryant for so long that she was completely left out! It just wasn't fair!

"Let's go, Carli!" shouted Auntie Michelle over the din. "We'd better make a move, otherwise we'll miss our bus."

With her head down, Carli shuffled out of the

Friends Forever

room. She was so relieved that her ordeal was over that she almost smiled. She couldn't wait to get home and back into her little bedroom. At the moment it was the only place in the world where she felt safe.

Chapter 7

Sunday dawned clear and crisp. Gemma spent the morning playing with Thumper in the garden. The big grey rabbit snuffled happily around the lawn, his shiny pink nose sniffing the grass still stiff with frost.

Gemma felt very anxious about going round to Sunita's. She'd spent half the night worrying, wondering what would happen if Carli *did* show up. While Sunita had been fine about the idea, she hated the thought of starting another argument with Lauren but at the same time, she was determined to befriend Carli.

As she stood there in the garden, she hardly heard her mum calling her from the kitchen. "Gemma! Gemma! What do you want for your lunch?"

Mrs Gordon came out into the garden to

discover Gemma so deep in thought that she hadn't even noticed that Thumper was trying to dig his way under next door's fence.

"Gemma, quick!" she called urgently. "Thumper is about to escape again!"

"Oh, rats," muttered Gemma to herself as she grabbed Thumper's white fluffy behind just before it disappeared.

"Sorry, Mum! I was miles away," she explained as she put her rather cross rabbit back into his hutch.

"I could see that! What's up?"

Gemma put on her best smile. She didn't want her mum to know anything about her argument with Lauren. "Oh, nothing," she answered, breezily.

"Right then, what do you want to eat? And don't say 'anything without eyelashes' or I'll go bananas!"

Mrs Gordon was fast running out of patience with Gemma's quest to stop eating meat. Yesterday, her daughter had even asked if the cheese on top of her toast was vegetarian. "She'll grow out of it," her husband had said. Mrs Gordon hoped he was right, if only to make meal times simple again.

At three o'clock prompt, the front door bell rang.

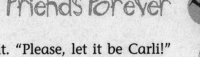

Gemma ran to answer it. "Please, let it be Carli!" she breathed. As she opened the front door, a look of disappointment crossed her face. It was Sunita.

"I thought I'd come and get you," her friend said with a grin, looking closely at Gemma's tense face as she slipped into the hallway. "What's up? You look like you've just lost a million quid!" Then it clicked. "No sign of Carli?"

"No," sighed Gemma heavily. "Wait a sec. I won't be long."

Five minutes later, the two girls were walking towards Sunita's house. "I still can't believe you actually went to the Fairlight estate on your own! My mum and dad would go mad if I went anywhere like that – specially without telling them. Gran would make sure I was grounded for a whole year!"

The girls went up the path to the neat terraced house. Old Mrs Banerjee answered the door and ushered them in.

"Your friend, Lauren, is already here but I think she's out in the garden talking to Vikram,"

chattered the old lady.

Gemma took a deep breath and Sunita squeezed her arm. "Don't worry, Gems. She'll be fine."

Mrs Banerjee had already put out some crisps on the table. "Mmm, great!" said Sunita, piling in. Just then, a familiar blonde figure bounced into the room, hair flying in all directions.

"Finished chatting up my brother, have we?" asked Sunita with a mischievous smile.

Lauren stuck her tongue out, playfully. "Hi, you two!" she cried. "Where's Anya?"

Gemma sat down on the sofa. "She's not coming Lauren, I told you yesterday – just before you stormed off."

Lauren looked crossly at Gemma, embarrassed that she'd brought the subject up in front of Sunita.

"Oh, you mean when I told you there was no way I was spending an afternoon with Carli 'boring-knickers' Pike, the biggest loser at Duston Middle School?"

Sunita, stunned at Lauren's tone, had to speak up. "How many times have we been through this?" she argued. "You shouldn't judge a book by its cover. That's what my mum is always saying to me."

"*Big deal*! I just don't want to be friends with her sort, all right?"

Sunita suddenly felt nervous. She thought that maybe she should warn Lauren now that Carli might turn up. Sunita hoped that it might soften the blow, but somehow, it all came out wrong.

"Well, you're not going to have much choice if she turns up this afternoon, and you'd better not be horrible to her," she blurted out without thinking.

"Pardon?" replied Lauren, clearly taken aback.

"*I* asked her," said Gemma boldly. "I thought that maybe if you spent some time with her, you'd change your mind."

Lauren stared furiously at the pair of them. How dare they? She wanted to say something, but she felt so angry nothing came out. She stood there with her mouth flapping like a goldfish.

"Well," she spluttered, "if you two would rather be friends with a nerd like Carli Pike, then you're welcome to her! Just count me out. Forget 'friends forever', I don't want to be friends with *either* of you two any more!"

Lauren stormed out of the living room, slamming the door behind her. Both Gemma and Sunita sat in silence. Tears welled up in Gemma's eyes. She and Lauren had never ever fallen out this badly before. "Oh, Sunita!" she began. "I was only trying to make everyone happy and look what's happened!"

Sunita hugged Gemma as she sobbed uncontrollably. "And I'm sorry I said what I did. I didn't really help, did I? Come on, Gems, Lauren's all hot air. It'll all be fine tomorrow, wait and see."

Gemma wiped her tears away with one of the paper napkins which had been laid out on the table for tea. She had never seen Lauren so angry or heard her say such things before. She wasn't so sure everything would be OK tomorrow at all.

Things weren't working out too well for Anya, either. It was nearly four o'clock, and her new friend Astrid still hadn't called to ask her over for tea. She plaited and unplaited her long dark hair impatiently.

"Right," she decided, as the clock in the hall chimed four, "I'm just going to have to ring Astrid and see if I can wangle myself an invite. I can't wait forever!"

Purposefully, she strode towards the lounge telephone and picked up the handset. Hearing the phone click, Mrs Michaels came in from her study to see what her daughter was up to. She frowned as she caught sight of Anya urgently punching in the numbers.

"Oh, hi, Mum," Anya tried to look as innocent as possible. "I'm just ringing Gemma to see if the girls are all meeting at her place today – I need some help with that maths homework!"

Mrs Michaels smiled back, proud that her daughter was so keen. "Just don't run up a huge bill, darling," she cooed. "Dad isn't made of money, you know!"

Anya frowned. What a load of rubbish, she thought to herself. As far as she was concerned, her dad was one of the richest ever. No one else in her class at school had a father with such an exciting job. Why, he got to meet all the big stars when he was making TV commercials.

"Hello?" came the whispery voice on the other end of the line.

"Oh, hi, Mrs Spencer, it's Anya. Is Astrid there?"

"Just one moment!" breathed Mrs Spencer.

A few seconds later, Astrid's polite tones came through the phone. "Hello, Anya. How are you?"

Anya could hardly wait to tell Astrid what had happened at the theatre the day before – with a few important details changed, of course.

"Hi Astrid! Guess what – something really mega

Friends Forever

Best Friends

happened yesterday. I met Claire Bryant and we got along brilliantly! She spent ages talking to me and said she really hopes we'll meet again when she visits our school!"

"Really?" came Astrid's cool reply. Although they'd only been friends a short while, it hadn't taken Astrid long to work out that Anya didn't always tell the truth.

"Oh yes, and she said she might bring Darcus Edwards with her as well. Isn't that totally *cool*?"

Astrid wasn't that impressed. As her father didn't allow her to watch much television, she hadn't a clue who these people were and why she should be as excited about them as Anya obviously was. She decided to change the subject.

"Well, things are getting very exciting here with the TV crew," she replied. "They made me walk in and out of Dad's studio five whole times yesterday! I didn't realise it would take so long – they say they're going to be around all next week!"

Anya decided that now was as good a time as any, and took a deep breath. "So, what are you up to this afternoon then?" she asked, crossing her fingers so tight that they turned white.

Astrid's reply was ice cool. "Oh, you know, not a lot. We like to just chill out, as Dad calls it, on Sundays."

"Oh, I'm not doing anything either," Anya said, brightly. She uncrossed her fingers and waited – surely Astrid would invite her round!

But, with a slightly bored air, Astrid simply coughed. "Got to go now, Anya, Mum's calling me. See you at school tomorrow. Bye!"

Anya could have cried. The rest of the day stretched out in front of her, long and empty. She wished now that she'd gone round to Sunita's house. At least her best friends would have listened to what she had to tell them!

"Oh, right," she stammered. "Yes, I'll see you tomorrow, then."

But the line was dead. Astrid had already hung up.

Chapter 8

Carli Pike had hardly been able to speak since her awful visit to the panto, and when her mum had told her of Gemma's visit, it had just made her misery greater still. She felt sure that now Gemma had seen her home, she'd be making fun of her today at school. Carli didn't know if she could face it.

Susie Pike sat down opposite her sad-faced daughter and sighed. "Are you feeling ill, Carli?" she asked, a concerned look on her face. Carli looked back at her mum and shrugged her shoulders.

"Well then, if you're not going down with something we'd better get you off to school, pet. You don't want to be late!"

Bundling Carli out of the door, Mrs Pike handed her a plastic lunchbox with Pocohontas on the front. "Come on, love. Annie will miss her school pick-up if we don't all get a move on."

Carli's expression didn't alter one jot, she just nodded.

"Will you be OK from here, love?" asked Carli's mum as they reached the top of Duston School's road. "Only we're a bit late, today..."

Carli just looked down at her scuffed shoes and muttered goodbye.

As she slowly dragged her feet along the pavement, Carli was suddenly aware of the sound of hurried footsteps behind her. The next thing she knew, someone had snatched the lunchbox out of her hand and had thrown it over her head. The sound of rough laughter greeted her ears as Alex, Marga and Charlotte surrounded her.

"So what do we have here, then?" sneered Alex. "Looks like bubbywubby's lunchy box!"

Alex threw the bright yellow container over to Charlotte who peered at it with disgust. "Ugh!" she said, pulling a face. "Did we pick up little sister's box by mistake then, fish-face? Here Marga – catch!" With that, Charlotte chucked the lunchbox at her mate, who was standing by the school railings.

Marga held her hands out, but the yellow box hurtled over her head, hit the railings, then fell

Friends Forever

onto the pavement, the lid breaking clean off. Alex and Charlotte fell about laughing, as Carli looked on horrified. Her mum had bought that for her birthday and she knew that there was no way she could afford a new one. She scrunched her toes up in her shoes in an effort to stop herself from crying, but it was almost impossible.

Alex strutted over to Carli and prodded the tiny girl with one big finger. "See that lunchbox?" she snarled menacingly. "Well, scab-features, if you don't do as we say, that could be your *glasses* next!"

A fat tear crept down Carli's cheek. She was terrified. Her heart was beating fit to burst. She looked up at the big girl pleadingly, but Alex simply laughed in her face. This was the bit she enjoyed the most, having the weaker girls at her mercy.

"Right, Pike," she spat. "This is the deal – you pay us a quid a week to keep you and your glasses safe, or else you know what'll happen."

"Yeah!" added Charlotte, who didn't want to be left out. "You'll get it!"

"Well, fish-face?" hissed Alex.

Carli's mind whirled. "I-I only get fifty p-pence a week pocket money!" she stammered. "I don't think I can manage a pound..."

Out of the corner of her eye, Carli could see

Gemma and Sunita jumping out of a car outside the school gates. For a split second, she thought about yelling out to them or running away, but then decided against it. No, she couldn't involve that Gemma Gordon again! 'I must remember what Mum told me,' she thought to herself, trying not to flinch as Alex stood nose-to-nose with her. 'Just walk away, *don't* rise to it...'

Alex was loving every second of it and even the shrill sound of the school bell didn't unnerve her. "Just remember then, *Loser*, that we'll be collecting your pocket money every Monday morning – or else. Come on, girls."

Alex signalled to Marga and Charlotte that it was time to leave – they'd done their work for the day. Without pausing, Carli bolted towards the school gates and through the big, blue doors.

All through the first lesson of the morning, Carli shook like a leaf. Even her teeth were chattering. Ms Drury came over to her table and looked at her closely, her face lined with worry.

"Are you cold, Carli?" she asked, kindly. "I know

that there's a bit of a draught from that window."

Carli quickly shook her head. She couldn't even look Ms Drury in the eye for fear of bursting into tears.

"No, Miss. Thank you, Miss," she mumbled, her voice as small as a baby mouse's.

Over the other side of the class, a battle of a different kind was going on. While Sunita and Gemma worked at their usual table, Lauren, who had swept straight past them without speaking, was now sitting with Tania and Katie.

Gemma stared sadly over at Lauren. She was already missing her oldest friend. Instead of grabbing a lift with the two girls that morning, she had cycled in by herself. The first Gemma knew of it was when she had gone to call for her friend, and Mrs Standish had told her that Lauren had already left.

"Leave her, Gems," said Sunita, with a sympathetic smile. "She'll soon get fed up with those two dimbos. I bet she'll be back by break!"

But the morning break came and Lauren showed no signs of coming round. Sunita and Gemma sat on the bench by the playing fields while Lauren hung around by the trees on the far side of the playground with Katie and Tania.

Gemma sighed. "I think maybe I should try and

talk to Lauren."

Sunita nudged her hard in the ribs. "Later, Gems!" she hissed. "Look – there's Carli, and she looks like she's been crying. Do you think we should go and see if she's all right?"

The two girls watched the slight figure in the flimsy cardigan hanging around the school doors. Her nose was the colour of a cherry tomato, and she clearly had tear stains on her cheeks.

Gemma hesitated for a moment, thoughtfully. "I'll go, you stay here."

Carli flinched as Gemma approached her, then, realising that it wasn't Alex back for another go, focused her eyes at the tarmac again.

"Hi, Carli!" said Gemma, as brightly as she could. "Did your mum tell you that you were invited to Sunita's yesterday?"

Carli sniffed hard as if she had a very bad cold and simply pushed past Gemma, without even looking at her.

Gemma couldn't believe it. Two people totally ignoring her on the same day. She walked back slowly to where Sunita was waiting.

"Well, what did she say?" enquired Sunita, looking puzzled.

Gemma shrugged her shoulders. "Nothing," she replied. "She just *blanked* me. Can you believe it?

First Lauren, and now Carli!"

Sunita frowned. She couldn't make any sense of it either. "Maybe she just wants to be on her own, Gems."

"No, it's more than that," replied Gemma quietly.

Sunita thought for a moment. "Do you think that Alex and her mates are stepping up the hate campaign? Maybe we should tell Ms Drury what's going on and let her sort it out."

"No, that won't work – look what happened the other week when I tried to help Carli. I got put in detention, Ms Drury didn't believe me!"

From across the other side of the playground, the school bell sounded. Sunita stood up and brushed her skirt with her hands in that decisive way she always did when she'd made up her mind about something.

"Right, only one thing for it then," she said firmly, her black eyes shining. "We need to get some firm evidence for Ms Drury."

"But how?" sighed Gemma.

"That," replied Sunita, catching hold of Gemma's arm as they walked across the playground, "is something we need to have a proper meeting about – but not now, maybe this weekend. I need time to think!"

Gemma knew that when Sunita had an idea, there was no stopping her. As the two girls walked back into the classroom, Gemma felt just a little better.

At Lady Margaret Regis School, Anya was having an altogether unpleasant time. Claire Bryant's singing class and lecture was about to take place and Anya, quite frankly, had lost her bottle. Normally upfront and talkative, she couldn't even get a squeak past her lips. As her class crowded into the music room, she felt sick and nervous.

"Right, girls," announced Mrs Daniels, the music teacher, "as you know, Miss Claire Bryant is coming here today – and the great news is that she might choose one of you to sing on her new CD, *if* you're good enough!"

Anya looked around at her excited friends and felt even more sick. She wasn't expecting this at all.

"All of you come and sit down over here. As soon as Miss Bryant arrives, we can get started," continued Mrs Daniels, fussing around the piano. "She's going to put you through your paces first, then she'll talk to you and answer questions."

"Wow! I hope I get chosen to sing with her," chattered Astrid, for once forgetting her composure. "Mum says that I've got perfect pitch, so I should be all right!"

"Lucky you!" said Jade. "My dad says that I sound like a drowning cat. But who'd miss the chance of meeting Claire Bryant?" she added, trying to hide her autograph book inside her jumper.

"Don't let Mrs Daniels see that autograph book," gasped Astrid. "She'll go ballistic! Anyway," she added, more calmly, "it's really not very cool to pester famous people, that's what my dad says."

"Isn't this great!" beamed Krista excitedly. "I can't wait! I'm really glad now that I practised all weekend! What about you, Anya?"

Anya tried to smile back at Krista, but found herself grimacing instead. She seemed to have lost all control of her face muscles and her stomach felt like a hundred butterflies were caught inside it.

The door to the sunny room swung open and in walked Claire Bryant. The girls instantly went silent and every pair of eyes in the room were fixed on the slight blonde figure in the leopard print dress. Claire was wearing knee high black boots and her shiny hair was held back by a black velvet headband. She looked every inch the star.

Mrs Daniels was all smiles. She almost danced on

the spot as she introduced their guest. "Now, girls, I'll leave you to Miss Bryant. Enjoy yourselves!" she chirped, backing into a corner of the room.

"Hello girls! I'm Claire," the beautiful young woman began, "would you mind introducing yourselves one by one please? We'll start with the girl with the long dark hair!"

Anya felt herself reddening as Astrid looked at her, enquiringly. After all, she'd boasted to her how well she'd got on with Claire backstage at the theatre, and now it became clear that Claire hadn't a clue who Anya was.

"I'm Anya Michaels," she said, her voice cracking and her face turning even redder.

One by one, the rest of the class introduced themselves. Claire smiled and nodded, then walked gracefully over to the piano.

"OK, girls, starting with Anthea, can you all sing this, please?"

Claire's long fingers tripped over the keyboard and played a scale. The silence in the room filled up Anya's ears as the notes died away. She coughed nervously.

"Anthea, dear," repeated Claire looking straight at Anya, "would you mind starting us off?"

The class tittered. Anya thought that this was the worst moment of her life. Not only had Claire

Bryant already forgotten her name, she was now making a show of her in front of her friends. Anya looked across at Astrid, who was watching her with an unmistakable sneer.

"Don't be shy!" said Claire, coaxingly. "Sing up!"

Anya cleared her throat and shakily began. But the notes wouldn't come out right, no matter how she tried. "La-la-la-LaaA*Aaah*!" she croaked, completely off key. It was true what her mother said about her – she was absolutely tone deaf.

Claire Bryant's face glazed over. She looked at the pile of papers on top of the piano and then looked again over at Anya.

"Anthea," she began softly, although the pained look on her face betrayed her thoughts.

"It's *Anya*, Miss Bryant," mumbled Anya, as red as a beetroot.

"Well, Anya – thank you, I think that's enough for now. Right, who's next?"

Anya was so embarrassed, her cheeks felt as if they were burning up. Out of the corner of her eye, she caught sight of Astrid and Krista shaking with silent laughter. She knew that she had blown her cool image with them, *big time*.

Chapter 9

The following week was really tough for Carli. Alex, Charlotte and Marga made sure that she realised their threats were not idle ones. On Monday, her English book was torn up and thrown away. On Tuesday, she found that her gym kit had been smeared with jam and mustard. Then, on Thursday, during science, Charlotte had jogged her elbow just as she'd picked up a test tube, making her drop and smash it all over her experiment work.

Sunita and Gemma had kept their eyes peeled all week for any firm evidence which they could bring to Ms Drury's attention. But Alex was too clever – there was absolutely nothing they could pin on her.

In the staff room, Ms Drury told Mrs

Mackintosh, the headmistress, that she felt that Carli wasn't settling in too well. "She seems completely uninterested in all the lessons," she confided to the stern, grey-haired headteacher. "And while she's not naughty, she really isn't putting in much effort."

"Is she making new friends?" asked Mr Coakley, Class 8's form teacher.

"I don't think so," sighed Ms Drury. "She seems to be a bit of a loner."

"I've had her type in my class before," said Mr Coakley, nodding thoughtfully. "Girls like that can be a bit off at first, but once she gets into the routine at Duston, I'm sure she'll be fine. Just give her some time to get used to everyone."

Mrs Mackintosh shook her head. "I'm not so sure with Carli, Mike. Perhaps a trip to my office might shake her into putting some effort in."

"Well," said Ms Drury, "I'll see what happens this week. I'll only send her if everything else fails."

In the classroom, things were still terrible between Lauren and Gemma. Lauren had refused to speak to either her or Sunita since the showdown on Sunday.

"Honestly, Sunita," said Gemma, running her hands through her bobbed hair, "I've tried everything. She just won't speak to me."

"Nor me," sighed Sunita. "And I couldn't believe it when she threw away that chocolate you left in her lunchbox the other day. It was her favourite too!"

Gemma looked so sad that Sunita could feel herself start to get upset too. She put her arm around Gemma's shoulders, comfortingly. "Gems, *I'm* still your friend – and so is Anya. When I spoke to her last night, she said she was going to ring you to cheer you up. Actually, she didn't sound that happy either – maybe you two can have a good old moan together!"

The two girls smiled at each other. Gemma felt glad inside that she could still rely on two of her best friends, but with Lauren blanking her completely...

She started to wonder – was looking out for Carli really worth it?

That weekend, Sunita decided to try and perk Gemma up by taking her shopping. First thing on Saturday morning, she called her.

"Hello?"

Friends Forever

"Gems, it's me, Sunita."

"Oh. I was hoping it might be Lauren," replied Gemma.

"*Thanks!*" said Sunita, undaunted. "Listen, what are you doing this morning?"

Gemma sighed. "Nothing really. I'm not dressed, yet."

"Right, it's decided. Mum is going shopping and you're coming with us. Don't argue, just get yourself ready and we'll be round in half an hour."

"But..." began Gemma.

"I won't take no for an answer," said Sunita, firmly. "See you later!"

By the time Mrs Banerjee reached the Whitecross shopping centre, it was packed out. The sales were finishing, and Northborough was full of bargain hunters.

After her mum had taken up an hour dragging the two girls into every household shop she came across, Sunita realised that her plan wasn't going to work.

"Oh, Mum!" complained Sunita as Mrs Banerjee walked into yet another shop full of rugs, candles and lampshades. "Can't we go and have a look in *New Girl*? They've got some great stuff in!"

But Mrs Banerjee was absorbed with a huge glass vase studded with what looked like multi-coloured marbles. "Look girls," she said, excitedly. "I've found just the thing for grandma's birthday. She'll love this!"

She took the big vase over to the cash desk, leaving Sunita and Gemma to rummage through the bargain bin. "Nothing much here," sighed Sunita.

"Why, fancy seeing you two here!"

Gemma and Sunita looked up over the bargain bin to see Mrs Michaels smiling broadly at them, with Anya and another girl in tow.

"Hi Anya!" beamed Sunita. "Wow! *Love* the coat!"

Anya smiled a little sheepishly, and dug her hands deep into the pockets of her furry dalmatian print jacket. Her black hair framed her face and fell over the collar beautifully.

"Thanks, Mum's just bought it for me."

The two girls smiled at the pretty, curly-haired girl in the green coat who stood next to Anya.

"And this is…?" enquired Gemma.

"Oh, sorry, this is Astrid. Astrid, meet two old friends, Sunita and Gemma."

So this was the famous Astrid. Sunita and Gemma exchanged glances – they couldn't help noticing that Anya looked just a touch uncomfortable.

"Hi, Astrid," said Sunita with a grin. "So, how is the filming coming along? Anya is so excited about being on TV, she's been telling us all about it!"

Astrid looked at Sunita with puzzled eyes. She opened her mouth to say something, but Anya jumped in.

"Oh, I might not *actually* be on television you know," she said quickly. "It all depends…"

Astrid looked at Anya enquiringly. She hadn't the faintest idea what she was on about.

"But I thought you said…" began Gemma, her brows knitting together.

Anya danced on the spot, her cheeks flushing as she hastily changed the subject. "So, Gemma, how is Thumper?"

Gemma looked at Anya as if she had gone mad. Anya hated rabbits! "Er, fine," she replied. "Anyway, did you find out if you got picked to be on Claire Bryant's new CD then? You seemed to think you would when you phoned the other night…"

Anya looked more uncomfortable than ever. She shifted on the spot and fiddled with the buttons on her expensive coat, her face getting

hotter by the second.

Gemma realised something was up with her friend. "Thanks for that call, by the way," she said, changing the subject herself this time. "You really cheered me up."

Astrid frowned. "But you didn't even..."

Right on cue, Mrs Banerjee returned with her wrapped purchase.

"Oh, hi Sacha!" she smiled at Anya's mum. "How lovely to see you!"

"Hello Indranee!" Mrs Michaels replied brightly, her pretty slavic features creasing into a brilliant smile. "It's so nice to see you too! But we have to dash now."

"Yes, we must *go*!" affirmed Anya through gritted teeth. Already, Astrid was looking cool and distant. Anya sensed that she was itching to leave.

"All right," said Mrs Banerjee, leading Sunita and Gemma out of the shop. "I'll call you soon, Sacha, and we'll meet up for a coffee."

"OK!" said Mrs Michaels, with a grin. "Come on, then, you two..."

"Phew, did you see Anya's face when you mentioned the TV programme and when I asked about the CD?" blurted Gemma as soon as Anya's party were out of earshot.

Sunita pulled a strand of hair away from her

eyes and frowned. "Well, I think we can safely say that Anya isn't going to be on TV *or* singing with Claire Bryant, don't you?"

Gemma shook her head and smiled, ruefully. "Poor Anya! It never seems to go right for her, does it?"

"Indranee!"

The two girls stopped dead in their tracks. There, outside the newsagents, stood Mrs Standish and Lauren. Mrs Standish went to kiss Sunita's mum on the cheek.

"Karen! Fancy seeing you here too!" Mrs Banerjee replied delightedly. "How nice that we've all met up!"

Lauren flushed, and looked as if she wanted to disappear into the ground.

Mrs Standish peered at Gemma. "Why, hello stranger! Where have you been all week?"

Gemma thought quickly. She certainly didn't want Mrs Standish to know that she and Lauren had fallen out.

"Oh, you know," she blustered, "Dad has been so busy at the garage that we've all had to lend a hand. Even Lucy!"

Mrs Standish looked at Gemma slightly oddly. "That's funny, Mary didn't mention it!"

Lauren kicked the toe of her boot against the pavement, while her mum chatted to Mrs Banerjee. She had to do something to get away from this, fast.

"Mum, we said we'd pick Ben up at midday and it's nearly five past. Shouldn't we be going?" she barked, without looking at her two friends once.

"Yes, we really must get a move on too," added Mrs Banerjee. "See you, Karen. Come on girls, let's go!"

Gemma looked at Lauren as they disappeared into the crowds. She felt a massive wave of sadness crash over her. She was really missing Lauren, and she knew Sunita was too.

"Come on, Gemma," said Sunita quickly. "We'll talk it through back at home."

Back at the Banerjees', Sunita's grandma was in full wail. As soon as Mrs Banerjee put the key into the lock of their door, the old lady burst into view, her hands in the air, wearing a frantic expression.

95

"*Beti*, where have you been?" she wailed, her steel grey hair escaping from the tightly curled bun on top of her head. "I have been so worried!"

Sunita's mum sighed. She was used to this routine. "There was no need to worry. We were only shopping!"

Mrs Banerjee Senior sighed so heavily that her whole body shook. "But look at this!" she replied, waving a crumpled blue envelope at them. "Look what that blasted postman did to this important letter from Delhi! He has ripped it to pieces forcing it through the letterbox and now I can't read it!"

The old lady looked as if she was about to burst into tears. She was getting herself in a real state.

"I think we'd better disappear and leave this to Mum!" whispered Sunita, beckoning Gemma upstairs.

Sunita closed her bedroom door and watched as Gemma slumped down on the bed, still shaken from their earlier meeting with Lauren.

"Are you all right?" asked Sunita. The pair could hear Mrs Banerjee wailing downstairs at the top of her voice.

Gemma nodded sadly and tucked her knees under her chin. "Yes, I'll be fine. But anyway, what are we going to do about Alex and her gang?"

Sunita opened the door of her wardrobe and

from the back of it, she pulled out a small black machine. "*This*," she said triumphantly, "is what we are going to use to get Alex Marshall once and for all!"

Gemma stared at the rectangular black box, and realised it was a Walkman. "What are we going to do, play tapes at her?" she asked, her blue eyes darting back and forth.

Sunita leant over to her desk and picked up a new blank cassette. "No, silly…" She opened the machine and put it in. "Ganesh gave this to me when he got his new ghetto blaster for Christmas. It's a *recording* Walkman! With this, we can get the evidence we need to prove that Alex Marshall is bullying Carli!"

Sunita held the tape recorder aloft, her eyes sparkling like black diamonds and continued, "Have you noticed how Alex always starts on Carli when she thinks no one is around?"

Gemma nodded. She had seen it for herself more than once.

"Well, all we have to do is to sneak up, tape Alex, and then take the recording to Ms Drury! It's simple! And best of all, the netball tournament is coming up on Wednesday, and I'll bet my Girls Together CD that Alex takes the opportunity to have a go at Carli!"

Friends Forever

Best Friends

Gemma gazed at her friend in wonder. Sunita was right. If they had a tape of Alex bullying Carli, then surely Ms Drury would believe them and do something about it?

Gemma took a deep breath. She held out her hand and linked little fingers with Sunita. The two girls looked deep into each other's eyes and repeated their secret oath.

friends forever, enemies never

"Right!" said Sunita, releasing her grip on Gemma's little finger. "That's settled then. At the tournament, we put our plan into action!"

Gemma took a deep breath. There was so much at stake – they *mustn't* fail.

98

Chapter 10

"Single file now, girls! Do hurry along, Amy. The netball tournament won't wait for us!" cried Ms Drury, a clipboard in her hand and a harassed expression on her face.

Outside the gates of Duston Middle School, two huge white coaches stood in the road.

"I can't see Lauren anywhere, or Carli," exclaimed Gemma, trying to warm her hands in her coat pockets. It was the coldest day since term began, and she'd forgotten her gloves.

Sunita scanned up and down the rows of excited girls. She could see Katie and Tania, and by the gate were Mabel and Laura. "I bet she's late, Gems. She'll turn up. In any case, we'd better get on board."

The two girls climbed the steps of the massive coach. It was plush inside – there was even a toilet on board! Pressed up against a window in the middle was a small figure, empty seats all around her.

"There's Carli," said Gemma, pointing at the blotchy-faced girl. Her eczema rash seemed to have got worse. "Hi, shall we sit with you?" offered Gemma, as she and Sunita moved towards the empty seats.

Carli eyed them both suspiciously. "No thanks," she replied stiffly. "I don't need your charity."

"Suit yourself," remarked Sunita, under her breath.

Then, just as the last few girls were getting onto the coach, Mrs Standish's old Ford Escort rocketed up the road. Lauren clambered out, looking worried and very nervous.

Sunita peered out of the coach window. "Look, she's here!"

Gemma craned her neck to see. She wondered where Lauren would sit. There was a spare seat alongside her and Sunita, but Lauren strode past them to join Tania and Katie. At the very back of the coach, Alex, Marga and Charlotte sat, sniggering. They were anticipating a fun day ahead of them – at Carli's expense. Carli hadn't paid up on Monday, and they intended to get their money's worth another way...

Half an hour later, the coaches drew up at Lutterworth Sports Centre. The car park was already choked with lines of buses filled with chattering girls.

As their coach unloaded, Gemma touched Lauren on the shoulder. "Good luck!" she whispered.

Lauren simply ignored her and walked off in the direction of the changing rooms. As she strode away, she couldn't help feeling rotten. Still, Gemma clearly put the feelings of a no-hoper like Carli before her best friend's. Even so, Lauren couldn't deny that she was missing Gemma badly.

The tournament was nail-biting. The Duston supporters clustered on the far side of the arena and went wild cheering their team on.

"Go on, Lauren! Get that ball!"

"Come on, Duston!"

The girls' shouts shook the block where they were seated. Everyone got to their feet and yelled themselves hoarse as Lauren scored for the third time.

"We've made it!" shrieked Sunita, as the full-time whistle went. "We're in the final!"

"Do you think we'll win? We're up against one of the toughest teams in the county," wondered Gemma, as Duston returned to the dressing rooms to rest before the final match.

"Right now, I'm more interested in where Alex Marshall and co have sloped off to," hissed Sunita behind her scarf. "I just saw her signalling to the others to go. We'd better follow them. Can you see Carli anywhere?"

Gemma's keen blue eyes scanned the rows of girls. In amongst all the navy and yellow uniforms, Carli had completely disappeared. Her heart skipped a beat. This was it, then!

"Let's go, Sunita! We mustn't lose them!"

The two girls squeezed in between the seats and into the gangway.

"And just where are you two going to?" came a stern voice. It was Mrs Mackintosh, the school headmistress.

Sunita thought quickly. "Gemma is feeling a bit sick, Miss, so we're going to the toilet."

Mrs Mackintosh eyed Gemma warily. "Yes, I suppose you do look a bit peaky. OK, but be quick. The game starts in five minutes and we need everyone to cheer the side on!"

"Phew, that was close!" breathed Sunita, as the two girls ran on. "Where to now?"

Gemma stopped in her tracks for a second to think. "Let's try the changing rooms! It'll be quiet in there and perfect for Carli – and Alex will know that too."

102

Sunita shivered.

"Not having second thoughts, are you?" asked Gemma.

Sunita smiled nervously back. "Of course not! I've just got butterflies, that's all!"

At last, the pair reached the changing rooms and gingerly pushed open the heavy door. They tiptoed inside and, together, crept along the rows of coats and lockers. Sunita motioned to Gemma to hush, and pointed to the end of the far row. There was Carli.

"What is she doing?" whispered Gemma.

The small girl was huddled under a coat, sketching away in a small yellow book. She was completely absorbed in what she was doing, her pencil making busy strokes on the page.

"Looks like our Carli might be a bit of an artist," said Sunita in a hushed voice. "She's a bit of a dark horse."

Suddenly the door was flung open so hard that it hit the wall with a loud bang. Carli started, nearly dropping her pencil.

"Well, well... what do we have here?" came a familiar, sneering voice. "So fish-face doesn't want to support our school with the rest of us, eh?"

From between the rows of coats, the unmistakable figure of Alex, followed closely by

Marga and Charlotte, appeared. Her face took on a menacing expression as she slowly rubbed her hands together.

"Quick, Sunita!" hissed Gemma urgently. "Start the tape recorder!" Sunita fumbled in her bag for a moment, then produced the machine. She pressed the red record button and shoved the Walkman as far through the row of coats as she dared.

Alex, Marga and Charlotte surrounded Carli. Alex poked the girl hard in the chest and Carli, terrified, lost her grasp on her sketchbook.

"You haven't paid up this week, and so *we've* come to collect," said Alex, menacingly.

"Oh, look at this!" shrieked Charlotte, delightedly. "Fish-features has been doing little piccies for her baby sister! Ugh! What a load of old rubbish!" With that, she tossed the sketchbook over the coat rack. It fell open with a dull flop at Gemma's feet.

When Gemma picked up the book, she could hardly believe that Carli could have done the incredible drawings she was now looking at. She quickly stuffed the book safely into her coat pocket.

"Well, then!" demanded Alex. "Where's my money, poo-face?"

Carli's bottom lip trembled. She tried to squash herself further into the coats, but she knew there was no escape. "I... I... haven't got it!" she wept, tears welling up in her sad green eyes. "I told you, I can't afford that kind of money."

Marga walked over to the small girl and viciously grabbed her arm, twisting it through her cardigan. Carli bit her bottom lip to stop herself crying out. She didn't want them to see that she was in pain.

Behind the coat rack, Gemma couldn't stand it any more. "We've *got* to go and get Ms Drury," she whispered to Sunita. "This is getting well out of hand! Look, you run and find her and I'll try and distract Alex. There must be enough on that tape to convince Ms Drury that this is serious."

"Are you sure?" replied Sunita warily. "Alex looks like she's going to get nasty."

"You're telling me! Now go on, *hurry*!"

Clutching the tape recorder, Sunita wriggled along the floor of the cloakroom until she reached the door. Opening it as silently as she could, she gave a thumbs up to Gemma and slipped outside.

Gemma took a deep breath then stepped out from her hiding place. "Oh, that's really hard, Alex," she said, as calmly as she could, hoping her knees wouldn't start knocking. "Bullying a girl smaller than you. You're so *tough*!"

Alex spun round. An angry flush spread over her greasy face. "Mind your own business, Gemma

Gordon!" she threatened.

Gemma drew herself up to her full height. She still only came up to Alex's ears. "Bullies like you should be *everyone's* business!" she said, defiantly.

Alex narrowed her eyes and clenched her fists. She walked slowly over to Gemma, her big, oily face alive with fury. When she spoke, her voice was low and harsh. "If you know what's good for you, Miss Busybody, you'll just butt out. Walk away and forget all about this."

Gemma looked Alex straight in the eyes, and swallowed hard. "Yeah? Just you try and make me!"

That was it. Alex grabbed Gemma by the collar and pushed her hard against the coat pegs. Gemma winced as one of them caught her in the back of the head. She could hear Charlotte and Marga laughing along with Alex.

"Huh! Not so tough after all, are you?" she scoffed. "Let's see if I can knock some sense into you."

But just as Alex grabbed a hank of Gemma's hair, the door of the cloakroom swung open, directing a chink of light onto the huddle of girls.

Charlotte and Marga were frozen on the spot. Alex turned round to see Mrs Mackintosh striding towards her, a thunderous expression on her face.

"Alex Marshall, stop that at once!" she bellowed.

Now it was Alex's turn to look scared. She

dropped Gemma like a hot potato, caught red-handed. Close behind Mrs Mackintosh stood Ms Drury and Sunita, who was out of breath and shaking.

In the corner, Carli was weeping silently. Ms Drury ran to comfort her.

"I think we're going to have to get your father in for a serious talk!" boomed Mrs Mackintosh to Alex.

Alex cowered – she was more frightened of her father than of anything else in the world. She knew what she was going to be in for.

Sunita was already right beside Gemma, who was resting on the bench, rubbing her sore head. "Are you OK, Gemma?"

Gemma smiled weakly and nodded. "A bit shaken, but I'm OK. Thanks for bringing the cavalry!"

"No probs," grinned Sunita. "Lucky we made it just in time."

Mrs Mackintosh turned her steely gaze towards Charlotte and Marga. "I think your parents will have to be informed, too. Ms Drury, take these three back to the coach immediately. I'll telephone their parents from the steward's office."

Grimly, Ms Drury marched the three girls out of the cloakroom. All of a sudden, Alex looked small and scared, her eyes shining with gathering tears. Gemma had never seen her rival like that before.

"Not so hard now, are you?" she muttered.

Mrs Mackintosh turned towards Carli. Her face softened as she looked at the small, red-faced girl. "Why didn't you tell us what was happening?"

Carli sniffed and shrugged. "Don't know, Miss. I thought you wouldn't believe me, and that if I told anyone, things would get worse."

Mrs Mackintosh put her arm around Carli's tiny shoulders and looked at the girl kindly. "Carli... at Duston, we always take any reports of bullying very seriously. If it happens again, you *must* come to me? OK?"

Carli wiped her nose on her sleeve and nodded.

"You're very lucky," Mrs Mackintosh continued, "to have such good friends as Gemma and Sunita. If it hadn't been for them, heaven knows how long this would have gone on before we'd have had proof that Alex Marshall had been ganging up on you."

Sunita and Gemma beamed at Carli. For the first time, the small girl smiled back at them.

Gemma walked towards Carli and took her arm gently. "*Now* can we be friends?" she asked.

Carli looked gratefully up at Gemma. "I never thought that anyone so popular would want to be

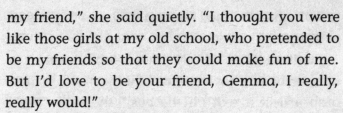

my friend," she said quietly. "I thought you were like those girls at my old school, who pretended to be my friends so that they could make fun of me. But I'd love to be your friend, Gemma, I really, really would!"

"Right!" said Sunita, dusting her skirt off decisively. "That's settled, then. You're in our gang, as from now!"

Gemma reached into her pocket and drew out Carli's sketchbook. She handed it over. "These are brilliant," she enthused. "I wish I could draw like you!"

Carli's face lit up. "My sketchbook!" she cried. "Thanks, Gemma."

Gemma opened her mouth to reply, but then hesitated. She had suddenly become aware of the cheering outside. It seemed to be getting louder and louder, reaching a fever pitch – just as a shrill whistle blew. The match was over.

"Quick!" she cried, running out of the door. "Let's find out if we won!"

Gemma ran along the corridor, straight into a crowd of decidedly down-hearted-looking Duston girls. Amy and Laura were nearly crying, and Katie stared down at her shoes miserably. No one was laughing or joking. Gemma's heart sank. Duston had lost.

Friends Forever

"Oh no," breathed Gemma. "Lauren is going to be *so* upset."

Sunita looked at her friend, who seemed to know exactly what she was thinking. "Let's go and grab a decent seat on the bus," she said. "We'll save a place for Lauren – she'll want cheering up."

"Do you think she'll even speak to me, Sunita?"

Sunita shrugged. "I don't know, Gems. But there's only one way of finding out."

Back on the coach, Carli shyly approached the two girls.

"Can I sit with you?" she asked, grinning, her green eyes sparkling behind her glasses.

"Oh, I think that just might be possible!" replied Sunita, smiling back, shuffling up to the window to make room for her.

As Ms Drury began the head count, the three girls sat together chattering, Carli proudly showing Sunita her sketches.

"I've never shown anyone these before," she said, a little shyly. "But as we're all friends now, you can look."

110

Just then, Gemma caught sight of Lauren. She could make her out quite clearly, two rows away, sitting with her head bowed. Taking a deep breath, she got up slowly, headed across to her, then touched Lauren on the arm.

Lauren hid her face. It was obvious she'd been crying.

"Lauren, I'm so sorry you lost," began Gemma. "Look, I'd like us to be friends again. Please. I can't *bear* this."

Lauren turned to face her. She paused for a second, then flung her arms around Gemma's neck. "Oh Gems," she cried. "I've been so silly and stubborn as usual. I'm sorry we fell out."

Gemma shut her eyes and returned the hug. Then she sat down beside her.

Lauren wiped away her tears with a tissue. "I heard what you did for Carli, it's buzzing round everywhere! I think you're really brave – both you and Sunita. I wish I'd taken the time to help too."

Gemma smiled at Lauren, and stretched her little finger towards her. Lauren sniffed back a big tear and meaningfully did the same. The two girls linked fingers and, together, repeated their special motto.

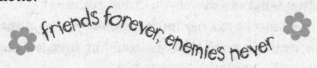
friends forever, enemies never

Sunita felt a lump in her throat as she watched her two best friends making up. She beamed at Carli, then breathed a huge sigh of relief.

"What a wicked day! This is better than if Duston *had* won the cup!"

The next evening, Mrs Gordon – who was delighted that her daughter was happy again – invited everyone to tea. She even made separate vegetarian food for Gemma.

In the kitchen, before they all arrived, Mrs Gordon took her daughter to one side.

"You know, your father and I are really proud of what you did for Carli," she said, handing over a brown package. "So we thought we'd give you this."

Gemma tore the brown paper off the parcel, to find a large book entitled *The Complete Quick and Easy Vegetarian Cookbook*. Inside were hundreds of recipes and lots of advice on how to make sure you kept a balanced diet if you didn't eat meat.

Gemma kissed her mum. She knew that it was her way of saying that she could be a vegetarian after all. She was thrilled to bits.

"Wow! Thanks Mum. This is brill!" she cried, cradling the book in her arms. "I can't wait to get cooking!"

Mrs Gordon laughed. "Just make sure you clear up whenever you do, Gems! Your dad took a lot of persuading before he agreed to this."

Just then, the door bell rang. Sunita, Mrs Banerjee, Vikram and Ganesh arrived first, then Lauren appeared with her mum, Ben and little Harry.

But it was Carli who was guest of honour, along with her mum and her little sister, Annie. As soon as Mrs Gordon opened the door to them, Mrs Pike let out a shriek of recognition.

"So it *is* you!" laughed Mrs Gordon. "Gemma told me about Carli and I said I thought we knew each other years ago when our youngest were babies!"

"Yes, that was a while ago, wasn't it? Annie's quite a little lady now," replied Mrs Pike, ushering Carli's sister inside.

Gemma's sister, Lucy, eyed the new girl for a moment, then decided that she liked the look of her. "Hi, Annie," she said. "Why don't you come up to my bedroom and see the new Barbie car I got for Christmas! It's brill!"

Annie's face lit up. She looked up at her mum. "Can I?" she asked, shyly.

Mrs Pike laughed. "Off you go, love. Just don't break anything!"

Just as the party was really starting to get noisy, the door bell rang again. Mrs Gordon went to the door and, seconds later, came back with a very subdued Anya and Mrs Michaels.

"Hi, Anya!" chorused Gemma and Lauren happily, turning down the stereo.

"You don't look in the party mood," said Lauren. "In fact, you look like you're about to go to the dentist!"

Anya cleared her throat and looked searchingly at her three friends. "Well... I've got something to tell you," she sighed. "I won't be on the TV show after all. Astrid chose another girl, and it made me realise that you're the best friends anyone could have! None of you would have done anything like that to me."

Sunita, Lauren and Gemma jumped up and all three hugged the tall, dark girl until she was breathless.

"Well, we've got a surprise for you!" announced Gemma, walking over to where Carli stood. "Meet the new member of our gang – Carli!"

Anya looked suspiciously at the girl in glasses, and almost backed away. Gemma saw that Anya was less than keen, and grabbed her by the arm, pulling her over.

"Carli was being bullied by that thug Alex Marshall, so we put a stop to it. I've asked Carli to join us from now on, so that she'll always be safe amongst friends."

Anya slowly looked Carli up and down – then an awful moment of recognition hit her. Carli was the girl backstage at the panto! Anya immediately felt guilty, and decided that Carli didn't look so bad. She also hated to hear of people being bullied by that nightmare Marshall.

Anya walked over to Carli and hugged her. "Welcome to the gang!" she cried, her blue eyes shining, kindly. "Any friend of Gemma's is a friend of mine!"

Carli beamed at her.

"Actually, we've met before," Anya added, looking a little embarrassed. "I saw you backstage at the panto. I spoilt the whole day for myself by getting jealous when Claire Bryant noticed you and not me."

"What? I was jealous of *you* for being so pretty and confident!" replied Carli.

The five girls stood together, exchanging glances. Gemma put out her little finger and the others did the same. Carli hesitated, she wasn't sure what she should do. Gemma smiled kindly at her. "This is our special sign, Carli. We do it to show we're best friends."

The small girl carefully offered one little finger to Gemma and the other to Sunita. Sunita linked with Anya, and Anya joined with Lauren who linked back with Gemma. The two old friends giggled at each other, realising how silly they'd been to fall out. Taking a deep breath, the five girls chanted their secret phrase.

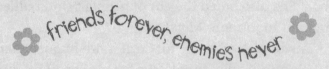

friends forever, enemies never

Now, more than ever before, the new group of best friends understood the meaning of those very special words. As they stood together in a circle, they each thought about what they'd been through in the last few weeks. Gemma, Lauren, Sunita, Anya and Carli all vowed silently to never let anyone come between them ever again.

OH BROTHER!

The half-term break has finally arrived. Anya plans to shop till she drops! Gemma's chuffed because she's been allowed to get another pet rabbit. Lauren just can't wait to play loads of football.

But the others are seriously depressed. Sunita's gran is threatening to organise a private tutor and no one can get a word out of Carli. The holiday gets even worse when Anya's half-brother Christopher arrives. Will the Best Friends manage to hold together?

Spotlight on SUNITA

When Sunita's attention is caught by a fashion competition on TV, she knows she has to enter. Problem is, she's also got to keep the whole thing top secret. Anya's out to win too, and has wangled the perfect headstart.

During the agonising wait for results, the other Best Friends have worries of their own. Lauren goes through torment when she tries out for the district football team, despite Carli's encouragement. And Gemma? Well, her little sister is driving her *mad*...

Best Friends

4

A Challenge for
LAUREN

Lauren goes pool crazy when she's selected as team captain for the annual swimming gala. But any celebrations are cut short when troublemaker Alex Marshall sets out to steal her place.

All the others want to help, but are never around at the right time. Gemma, Carli and Sunita land in trouble when a helping hand turns sour and Anya's swamped by unwanted clothes! Will the Best Friends be there when Lauren needs them most?

More brilliant Best Friends books available from BBC Worldwide Ltd

The prices shown below were correct at the time of going to press. However BBC Worldwide Ltd reserve the right to show new retail prices on covers which may differ from those previously advertised in the text or elsewhere.

All BBC titles are available by post from:
Book Service By Post,
PO Box 29, Douglas, Isle of Man, IM99 1BQ

Credit cards accepted.
Please telephone 01624 675137 or fax 01624 670923.
Internet http://www.bookpost.co.uk
or e-mail: bookshop@enterprise.net for details.

Free postage and packaging in the UK. Overseas customers: allow £1 per book (paperback) and £3 per book (hardback).